2010

For the Dunlops...

My first piece of fiction!

Enjoy!

Love,
Cat

MAMY WATA

By
Patricia Lee

Order this book online at www.trafford.com
or email orders@trafford.com

Most Trafford titles are also available at major online book retailers.

© Copyright 2010 Patricia Lee.
All rights reserved. No part of this publication may be reproduced, stored in a retrieval system, or transmitted, in any form or by any means, electronic, mechanical, photocopying, recording, or otherwise, without the written prior permission of the author.

Printed in Victoria, BC, Canada.

ISBN: 978-1-4269-3111-6 (sc)
ISBN: 978-1-4269-3112-3 (dj)
ISBN: 978-1-4269-3113-0 (e)

Library of Congress Control Number: 2010905554

Our mission is to efficiently provide the world's finest, most comprehensive book publishing service, enabling every author to experience success. To find out how to publish your book, your way, and have it available worldwide, visit us online at www.trafford.com

Trafford rev. 8/16/2010

 www.trafford.com

North America & international
toll-free: 1 888 232 4444 (USA & Canada)
phone: 250 383 6864 ♦ fax: 812 355 4082

Dedicated to my husband, Dr. Paul Fougère, for his editorial support.
Cover photograph donated by Dr. Herbert M. Cole, Santa Barbara, California
(From his personal collection)

CHAPTER 1

SLOWLY TURNING OFF I-25 FOLLOWING the map through New Mexico. Julia pressed her foot to the accelerator. Out of the corner of her very green eyes she caught the one and only lonely sign pointing east. Laughing to herself, Julia asked aloud how on earth that literary villain, Moriarity, Sherlock Holmes nemesis, had ended up on the desert in the southwest of the United States. Indeed, how had she? Her normally burnished brunette hair felt gritty from roadside dust so a few campsites back Julia had made a single braid out of her shoulder length hair. Almost at journey's end, she had gotten by the last few days of driving across the deserts from Los Angeles with cat baths, and she was looking forward to a hot shower when she reached the hacienda 30 miles south of Santa Fe. This is where Dominique now lives, and where they had chosen to rendezvous.

Wearing only blue denim shorts and a plain white T-shirt layered with a cotton Guatemalan vest with colors of striped persimmon and violet tones, her almost bare foot pressed harder on the gas pedal. Julia's shapely legs showed very brown stubs of fluff needing a shave but her petite feet—set in grungy leather thong sandals poked out with toenails painted the color of tangerines. In the deepening shadows of the day, Julia's face was bronzed from the sun and she looked like a Native American with very high cheekbones.

The Painted Desert that spread before her was incredibly beautiful as the fading light between the powerful Sangre de Cristo Mountains gave a lunar-like quality to the scene stretched out as far as her eyes could see. Julia was mesmerized by the monolithic buttes surrounding her. The canyons seemingly stood as sentinels against the vast expanses of sky—sprawling upward in a celestial magnificence smeared like a Revlon lipstick in a red jet streak. Gray funnels of clouds billowed upward meeting silver puffs of thermal spirals. It all suggested tribal campfires telegraphing smoke signals by the beating of drums. Entranced by the sunset, Julia's eyes were still alert to the road even though she could see out of one corner of her eye a sliver of moon that had suddenly etched the silhouette of a cowboy sitting tall in the saddle riding off, of course, alone and into the sunset.

"Welcome back to Hollywood" said Julia out loud. "I would not be at all surprised if they find me." Never one to feel daunted in a mission she shrugged the thought off and started to sing her own lyrics to the old tune: "All by myself alone… da de dum—onward into the sun."

Of all the women in the world, Julia was the last one to think she would ever be "on the run" or in a dangerous situation or at the epicenter of a worldwide bunch of thieves. Since meeting and falling in love with William Brewer her life had turned topsy-turvy. Just the thought of what had transpired since she left Africa made the woman breathe rapidly. A meditative type,

Julia automatically started reciting her mantra and focusing on her breaths--in out in out. She could feel the tensions subside from the tight muscles in her neck. Road weariness was settling in. Yet, her disciplined mind quickly focused on the road ahead. On the final lap of her trip, Julia deftly shifted her tired butt and sat up straight at the wheel with a force of willpower.

As the daughter of an art historian, Julia understood what went into creating a good painting and as she drove towards her destination on this remote but beautiful desert highway she wondered how to paint the scene before her without it becoming too garish. She thought of the hot shower and Dominique's wonderful manservant who also served as a cook, and she laughed at the way he and Banti and Julia had taken Mamy Wata right out of the museum. They were arriving from respective origins and the plan was set to get Mamy Wata back to Africa as soon as they safely could. Mamy Wata was now covered up in the back of the rented Cherokee Jeep, and Julia was looking forward to sharing the story with all of her colleagues at dinner.

• •

Dominique Chantel had come across the old hacienda after wandering around the area following the start-up of a new art gallery in Santa Fe. She had established galleries in Africa, Europe, and Morocco and now in the United States of America. She had created a lovely sanctuary near Santa Fe, New Mexico with a warm and nurturing environment that she had turned into a Bed & Breakfast retreat holding only 12 rooms. Many of the rooms have fireplaces and each of them have a charming, southwest motif with Georgia O'Keefe paintings on the walls and hand-woven Navajo rugs on terracotta floors. Situated on eight acres, the retreat offers a pool, ancient cottonwood trees, sauna and hot tub, as well as a stable with horses and an orchard. Dominique has an excellent chef serving both a French and a Spanish cuisine. Julia could not wait to see what would be served for dinner. She estimated about 45 minutes left before reaching the hacienda.

***

"Every woman should have a kitchen man," Dominique said to her dinner guests. "The meal you just finished is a major reason why I want to keep Louis Napoleon close by whatever quarters I am living in. Besides that, as you all know, he has been with my family since I was a child. I could not function without Louis. He is more than a chef that is for sure. He is even more than a manservant or a Man Friday. He is part and parcel of my family."

"His tangine was particularly good tonight," said Banti. "Perhaps that is because I so like when it is cooked in the traditional way in a clay pot over coals and the stew had such a nice tang of fresh lemons, fresh coriander, and home-cured olives. The couscous was mild---that made a nice contrast."

"Tonight, though," said Dominique, "he used chicken because, after all, we are on the desert and fresh fish is hard to find unless it is frozen."

"Well, you know very well, Dominique, that people from Boston cannot abide frozen fish," said Arthur Nolan, who was Julia's publisher and also a financial backer in their enterprise. Arthur had flown in from Boston, and responded to Dominique as he accepted an espresso of Moorish coffee.

Julia lay back on the love seat overflowing with brightly woven pillows and felt the warmth of a fire sitting near the southwestern stove and chimney made out of terracotta clay. The desert evening brought coolness to all, and Julia was content to simply be after the long and tiring trip. She felt clean from an elegant shower and soak in the hot tub, and now in a pair of Dominique's Moroccan style lounging pants and tunic, she easily could have purred like a cat as she sank back into the cushions and listened to her friend's conversation.

"Well, Julia, are you ready to tell us how it all went? According to plan?" Arthur asked.

"If it had not been for Louis, we could not have pulled it off. The whole drama went according to plan. I was not fully sure of my acting ability when we used the diversionary tactic. But the museum staff fell for it and that was what we wanted. Standing on the other side of the gallery, Banti was in her traditional dress with her flowing caftan and stood behind Mamy Wata; so that when I swooned and everyone gathered around me, no one even noticed Louis dressed up in those janitor overalls. He simply swept in and put the sculpture in the trashcan and wheeled it right out the back door. As the EMT's worked over me, Banti met Louis with the jeep and transferred Mamy Wata into it and they drove off. I can't imagine anything easier. And, once I told the support staff that I thought that I might be pregnant because I seemed to be fainting a lot lately, and especially in the morning before lunch, they were very conciliatory and suggested that I see my doctor right away. Fortunately, I was able to leave through the front door before any alarms went off or anyone noticed the missing sculpture. I met Louis and Banti two blocks away at a MacDonald's on the way to the airport, and drove them right to LAX. Then, I stopped to change my clothes and headed East off the freeway. That was the long and the short of it."

"Now it's time to examine her to see if she is in good condition." Banti rose to go and bring the statue in from the car. Everyone gathered around the large round coffee table and Banti put Mamy Wata on top of it. "You know, they had the temerity to tag her as the Black Venus. These are titles by which African masterpieces have been known since Pablo Picasso, Andre Derain, Maurice de Vlaminck, and Henri Matisse were among the many artists who collected and studied African sculpture. It really is not known how many of those pieces were stolen. It is well known in the art world that there is enormous profitability for stealing and smuggling our art and artifacts. So many dealers and collectors are willing to sell our artifacts into first world cultures. It seems to be part and parcel of a complicity that goes all the way back to Lord Elgin and the marble statues he stole from the Parthenon. Indeed, back to the Romans who looted Greek culture and brought it all back to Rome."

They stopped the conversation to look at Mamy Wata. Standing 24 inches tall she represented both the power and the wrath of the African goddess. He hair was black raffia and looked rather wild. She had bulging eyes and a full figure with pointed breasts. What was frightening and fierce about Mamy Wata was the cobra snake wrapped around her neck. The dark hardwood contrasted with a vibrant red palette around her lower body with a strategic use of contrasting textile patterns etched into the wood. Her hands reached out in a grand and gracious way as if demonstrating her active intermediary with the divine. Around her waist was a pocketbook made of cowry shells. Banti started to explain to Arthur their significance. "Cowry shells are used by our diviners for readings. Usually twelve shells are tossed onto a mat to read. If they see health, longevity, and prosperity, we call this wassa. Many of the folks in my region believe that the ancestors are very angry at post-colonial Africa. The proof is all around us. It is as if the ancestors have pronounced a curse. What is the sin, you might ask? It is the compact between Africa and the 20th century. It is an attempt to "modernize" without consulting cultural continuities—it is the attempt to "de-Africanize" Africa."

Mamy Wata

"Look at the mess we are in as a whole Continent. Bewildering military coups and economic shifts as a result of colonialism and the Diasporas. Large-scale corruption, collapses in foreign aid, disease, wars between the tribes and a war on cultures. We are still in a war between indigenous Africa and the forces of Western civilization. Inefficiencies, mismanagement, decay of infrastructures, well, I could go on and on."

She did. Banti went on to explain that it was her belief that the ancestors have been aroused from the dead, disapproving of rulers and the West. She felt it paramount that Africans find their identities and to do that they need to consult the ancestors as well as to pay attention to Africa's past with slave trades, territorial imperatives, a Eurocentric worldview, and urbanization into smaller and smaller spaces. "This push towards militarization and privatization comes from the whole Milton Friedman theory of economics and the chaos factors that have destroyed so much of third worlds. Then, on top of all that, she continued, there was an ongoing war between Islam and secularism. This is why Mamy Wata is so important. We need to ask: 'How can the ancestors be appeased?' This is an imperative because we need to look both inward as well as outward, and looking inward will root us in our heritage of the ancestors, especially now that the whole world has become a village. We need to germinate the seeds and seek our roots in our educational programs. Before a seed germinates it needs to decay and this is the stage Africa has been in since the end of the colonial rule. I hope that a new Africa may be able to re-germinate if we draw the best of our past heritage and use our present and future opportunities more wisely."

"You know, Arthur, " Banti said, addressing her remarks to the publisher with whom she was now working, "the theology of being one with nature is very much a part of the African worldview. We've always had a concept of God as being decentralized and not necessarily in the shape of Man. It is a primeval and universal power of the Spirit and it speaks to us with the ancestors as the intermediaries. In this time of global warming the Western view of power over the universe will need to yield to the power that comes from within. To be sure, totemism may be obsolete for the majority. But the essential philosophy of the continuity between man and nature more and more brings us to review the supernatural. We do so in terms of it being part of all the different elements in nature as experiences with God. It seems to many of us that the problems of Islam and Christianity and the Hebraic traditions are continuing to be the hot spots around the world. Besides, indigenous cultures in Black Africa are oftentimes matrilineal and even matriarchal. That's why female belief systems are beginning to re-emerge. This is the core of our teaching. We need to develop women's consciousness and the plight of women on the Continent."

Banti was about to go on when Dominique interrupted.

"Hold it, Banti," suggested Dominique. "Julia is really tired. I suggest that we meet in the conference room after breakfast and you can practice your lecture for the new educational series we've been working on. You've given Arthur quite an overview and he will be the perfect student for a Western mind being introduced to our curricula."

"As Banti has explained, " Dominique summarized, " the connection between the Spirit World and what is now going on to reclaim the roots of Africans, and especially women in the postcolonial Africa. This is the core of our teaching. We've been developing an online course about women's wisdom and the way of the elders. Perhaps colonial tyranny has not altogether left Africa, but simply changed its face with the new globalization issues. Still, it is a fact that Africa's raw materials continue to be exploited by western powers. We are trying to bring the best of the old ways into modernity, Arthur. So we are using Mamy Wata as the symbol of the old traditions of the ancestors. Westerners would no doubt call a Mamy Wata the symbol of shamanism and that it is a magical world. Owerri women beg to differ and this is what the lecture will help to explain. So, if it is agreed, let's say goodnight and meet tomorrow for the first lecture. In the meantime, I will ask Louis to clean up the sculpture and to check to see that nothing has been done to hurt her wood."

Everyone agreed to this plan and all said goodnight as Julia was very gratefully led to her bed and the first full sleep enjoyed in some time.

• •

When they entered the conference room after breakfast, Mamy Wata stood at the head of the table and Louis was sitting there beside Dominique.

"Good morning, have a seat. We brought more coffee on the side table. You are going to be astonished at what Louis has to show us. Sit; sit…" she flourished her hands toward the cushioned seats around the teak table.

"Louis, the floor is yours."

Louis stood up and drew Mamy Wata closer to his reach. "What I'm about to show you might explain why someone is after Julia." He reached behind the cowry pocketbook and lifted it up for all to see. "When I was examining her last night, this is what I found."

Everyone moved in closer to the table. Holding a sketcho pen Louis stuck it into the wood and out popped a piece as if on a spring lock. "It's a secret drawer, and wait until you see what is hidden inside it." Louis put the knife into the hole and drew out some something wrapped in cloth. He laid it on the table and everyone gasped when he opened the cloth. A diamond almost the size of a walnut lay before them. The room went totally silent. Arthur was the first to speak. "What do you suppose it's worth?"

"A most practical question, Arthur," spoke up Dominique. "Until it's appraised I don't think we have an earthly idea. Better yet, the next question might be—how did it get there—and why smuggle it in this way?"

"But that's not the half of it," said Louis. "Do you know what the diamond is wrapped in?"

"It looks like some sort of a map?" asked Banti. "Is it? What is it?"

"I am no scientist—that I know. If I am correct, I think it is some type of written code."

Everyone was dead silent.

They looked at what was on the table and then all turned to Julia to get her reaction. "I am as overwhelmed as you," Julia said, "but at least I better understand what has been happening. Why would they want to hide this inside the sculpture?"

"I think," Arthur, suggested, "that they might have thought if they let them sit in a museum and cool off (if you will)—well, nobody would think such a valuable item would be hidden inside an African sculpture. What we need to find out, if we can, is who was behind the consortium to bring this exhibit into the L.A. County in the first place? I think we have to start there."

"We?" interrupted Dominique. "Our mission was to get Mamy Wata back to Owerri, and now this opens a whole new kettle of fish. I think we need to get some expert in on this."

"What kind of expert do you have in mind?" asked Arthur, always the pragmatist.

"I think that I know what Dominique is talking about," said Banti. "You mean my brother, don't you Dominique?" as she turned to look directly at the woman at the head of the table.

"Yes, I do. Perhaps it is time that you tell everyone here exactly what you've shared with me about who your brother is and what he does?"

Eyes turned back to Banti. "My brother is the top undercover investigator for my country under the Ministry of Artifacts and Treasures. His name is Ketu Tutuoa, and if you've heard his name it is most likely in literary circles in Africa."

"Of course," exclaimed Arthur putting on his publisher's hat, "he is one of the more controversial figures in African literature. He has written a lot about these spirits you are referring to when you speak of Mamy Wata. There has been some criticism about his works but he is undoubtedly a vibrant and evocative storyteller. This is your brother? And you are now telling us that he also is an undercover agent in Owerri?"

"That is precisely what I am saying."

Julia spoke up and decisively said to Banti, "Can you contact him and how quickly can we get him to New Mexico?"

"I'll get on it right away."

Julia looked at Louis whose face appeared baffled. "What are you thinking?" asked Julia.

"I've been reading a lot lately about the smuggling operations that have been going on with the "blood diamonds" and also something about stolen gold. It's all rather complicated and I don't know if we are all in some sort of danger because sooner or later they are going to figure it out. Especially if we take Mamy Wata back to Owerri."

"Some analysts involved with the Gold World Trade Consortium say that diamonds and gold could ramp up with production because of the world's economic slowdown."

"And what I know from my brother," Banti added, "is that the so-called "blood diamonds" have been used by rebel groups to fuel brutal wars in Africa. These conflicts have resulted in over 4 million deaths and the displacement of millions of people. We are working with Amnesty International and a group called Free Trade for Diamonds to organize grassroots human rights organizations. We need to educate the public about the problem and we've been pressing governments and industry to take action. A large coalition of NGO's has launched a program to stop trade in conflict diamonds. We need to continue to ensure that governments pass national laws by policing itself with a system of warranties. But it isn't fully implemented. I suspect that the smuggling has increased before the laws are passed. The governments need to start periodic spot checks of diamond companies to make sure they have systems in place to prevent any trade in conflict diamonds. A rock this size would certainly not go un-noticed with the high profile of these issues. I know that other governments in Africa are participating in the so-called Kimberley Process. This is a program to launch an aggressive, multi-million dollar PR campaign aimed at convincing the public and to stop diamonds from fuelling conflict. Also, to protect the legitimate diamond trade in Africa. Industry profit and inaction come at the expense of economic development on the Continent and at the expense of people's lives. We know that many diamond-rich countries are extremely poor and people are not benefiting from the wealth in their soil. Diamond fields are rife with chaos and instability, and rebel groups and terrorists can still take advantage and access diamonds. The Kimberly Process means little to smuggling syndicates nor do they care about the hundreds of thousands of men and children digging for diamonds in dangerous, dirty and difficult conditions in Africa. They often earn less than a dollar a day from artisan mining, carried out with simple picks, shovels and sieves. All of this is what my brother has been working on. This, and the smuggling of artifacts and other valuables literally stolen out of Africa."

Dominique, who was the manager par excellence and kept everyone on track, spoke up. "We have enough issues here to keep us going throughout the day and into the night. I am wondering if the next immediate question, are we all safe here? Obviously, there is something going on that we've been extremely naïve about. What do you suggest we do in the meantime?"

"First of all," said Arthur, "we need to get this stone into a safety deposit box and I'm not sure what we do with this code. Perhaps we should also put it in the bank until Banti's brother has an opportunity to study it. I can't think where else to stash it, can you?" Looking at Dominique he asked if it was easy enough to go to a bank in Santa Fe. "Perhaps you and Louis could do that today?"

"Yes, of course, and secondly, as we planned--is it safe to move forward now and get Mamy Wata back to the village? Especially under these circumstances?" Dominique asked this open-ended question to everyone in the room.

The room again went quiet while everyone thought.

"Maybe," spoke up Banti, "well, maybe Julia should just go to Maine to her family's summer place as we'd planned and simply take Mamy Wata with her? To hide the sculpture until we know more? No one would find them up on the island of Vinalhaven, would they?"

Everyone looked around the table to consider this proposal. "Julia, what do you think?" asked Dominique.

"Let me consider all of this and I'll give you my answer after lunch. I need time to think. You know that I have to go to Boston to see my father, and my inclination is to head right back to Owerri as soon as I can. But let me think this all through."

"Okay. Then Louis, you and I will take these into the bank and we'll get back together early afternoon. Banti, get a hold of your brother as soon as you can and let's wait for his advice."

They looked a bit stunned as Louis wrapped the sculpture up in an Indian blanket and they filed out of the room---all in total silence.

CHAPTER 2

TO GET OUT OF THE longshoremen atmosphere of Chelsea, Massachusetts—just outside the City of Boston and in the bowels of the City's infrastructure where the workers lived---the population who actually kept the City going as contractors, bus and taxi drivers, Mass transit employees, and the like, William Brewer, known all his life as BB—knew from his teenage years that he wanted to live on the other side of the Mystic River. His path out of Chelsea was similar to the one his father had taken—only BB had his sights on something higher than an able seaman. Early on, BB decided he would become an officer in the Merchant Marines because what he had learned around the shipyards and working summer jobs as a "wharf rat" was that the sea could be the channel to take him far and wide. His goal was to get that officer's ring and eat in the ship's wardroom. During his senior year in high school, he was fortunate to find a job as a launch-man at a prestigious yacht club on the North Shore of Boston. During that summer he saw how the other half lived, and he wanted to become a member of the club.

Chelsea was a blue-collar town situated beneath the Mystic Bridge that led to Logan International Airport; and it was a port for cargo and container ships as well as a depot for the oil that came into the Port of Boston. Chelsea was a city of immigrants, especially the Sicilians who came to work in the factories at the turn of the 19th century.

In some ways, the Brewers' were misfits and especially BB's parents who seemed to be mis-matched in their marriage. Neither of them was afraid of the work ethic, and this was instilled in their son. They lived in a two-family wooden house—respectable and not a tenement; but decidedly located in a blue-collar neighborhood. BB's father worked at the shipyard as a welder, and he was proud of always paying his bills on time. Helen Seward Brewer came from nearby Winthrop and her people originally hailed from Nova Scotia. They were all hardy seafaring people and the women had mostly gone into the teaching profession. Winthrop, itself, had been a solid summer resort before they built Boston's Logan airport so Helen always felt herself to be a social notch above BB's father. Helen had attended a local Normal School and was a fourth-grade teacher. Helen and Will Brewer had met at a local school dance, and BB was their only child. Thus, BB became the center of Helen's universe. Every cent she saved went to him, and she always called him William. She would take him in on the subway to the Boston museums and she always read good children's literature aloud to him. Helen kept a clean house and insisted that her husband change for dinner from his blue overalls at the end of a long and tiring day. Helen had standards and always set the kitchen table with cloth napkins and candlesticks, even if they were just having American Spaghetti for supper. These values rubbed off on BB but it was from his father that he learned the love of the sea.

BB's best friend came from a Sicilian family and while BB was a dreamer, Geno was definitely a fellow of the streets---one of the guys. Geno's father was alleged to be involved somehow as a bookie in local rackets. The boys met on the football field and became fast friends. No matter how their lives were to diverge, they always kept in touch and throughout the years continued their business relationships that had begun when they were young men. BB loved to go over to Geno's house as his mother generally had a large pot of Italian home made spaghetti sauce simmering; or a fish fry because the cousins were fishermen out of Gloucester and the family was well supplied. Geno had confided with BB that he thought his cousins were involved in dope smuggling, and that they brought it in on the fishing boats. Being an only child, BB enjoyed the rough and tumble of Geno's large family and they, in turn, had embraced BB into the inner sanctum of their extended clan They always knew that BB was different and that he would go in a direction that Geno would not follow, but no matter. Geno's family was well connected with local politicians and they were able to open doors for BB so that he was readily accepted into the maritime academy when he applied in his senior year.

BB was a tall fellow and women really were attracted to him. He had a strong and very masculine physique. He and Geno worked out at the local gym and so they both stayed fit and filled up with masculine brawn. Still, it was BB with his wily black curls contrasting with sparkling blue eyes under dark lashes that caught the girl's eyes. BB was also the football team's quarterback and he was very agile at not getting sacked. However, he was not all that interested in the local girls. He had seen some of the beauties at the yacht club in the summertime, and he'd already made up his mind that he was going to follow class.

It was Geno's cousin, Sal Vitori, who introduced them to the racing track in nearby Suffolk Downs, and they quickly learned how to place a bet against the odds, especially when they got inside tips from Sal's father. BB—the more prudent one—having learned to save from his mother, protected their earnings; and slowly the little pot grew so that by the time high school graduation came around, they decided to start out as partners with Sal in foreign car mechanics. Geno had always wanted to get into racing cars; and he particularly was interested in BMW motorcycles from Germany. For the long term, BB promised Geno that once he started in the merchant marines he would send money to a saving & loan account they'd established and together they would be involved in building the business with BB as a silent partner. Little did he know what the growth potential would be as the investment continued to bear fruit.

If someone described BB, perhaps they might see how his intellectual side was evolving and it was this cross-wiring between the all-American hunk from the streets of Chelsea mixed with an aura of another world in the distance that gave him a mysterious twist that no one could really figure out. He was a man on the go, and he knew that the first step was to get an officer's ring and to gain experience by seeing the world. This self-confidence made people take notice and even Geno was astounded as to where it would take his friend. What, one was curious to know, led William Brewer ultimately to the office of Henry Seton Chilton, and into the life of Julia Chilton?

• •

After he finished his studies at the maritime academy, BB shipped out and this led him to many foreign ports and a lot of wild living. He continued to send stipends to Geno and the money was always deposited into their joint bank account; but he left the business side entirely up to his friend as he lived his adventures and learned to navigate on seas in faraway places. So it was another piece of luck that through his commanding officer on his final billet with the merchant marines that he met James Vogel. In civilian life, Vogel was a college professor at Columbia University in New York but during the latest national conflict he had been called up as a reservist to serve his country yet again to convoy goods and equipment and troops into troubled zones. Vogel could see that BB had natural talents and when they shared a cup of coffee in the wardroom, they would talk. BB had mentioned to Vogel that when this tour was over he wanted to contact some graduate schools. Vogel told BB to look him up if he made it to Columbia in New York City.

BB applied and did get admitted into Columbia but halfway through the first year, disaster struck like a summer squall. He was put on academic probation and was within a single percentage point of being tossed out. The problem was that he had met a woman who was gorgeous, but sexually draining of his time and energy. He originally thought he'd go for an MBA but the courses bored him. He felt that through Geno, he already knew enough about business, especially, from what Geno had told him about how easy it seemed to make a lot of money. So at the suggestion of his roommate he decided to look into the humanities.

"Oh, it's simple, Brewer," said his colleague when they got together one night for a beer. A spoiled preppie from Groton School, he said to BB: "Get smart like me, for Christ sake, and go into art history. The lectures are fascinating and you can snooze as soon as the lights go out and they show all their art slides. Art history is easy to grasp—memorize the slides and photographs then bullshit your way through, and you've got it made. Besides, you meet a helluva' lot of people in the art world. And you know what they say, it's not what you know but whom you know."

BB thought about the times his mother had taken him to the Boston art museums and how much he had enjoyed those excursions. So, he contacted Vogel and signed up for one of his classes. It was Primitive Art 101. Within a few sessions he found himself diving into the dark continent of Africa and became fascinated with the subject before him. Vogel was actually a trained anthropologist and as soon as he stalked down the aisle of the lecture hall toward the lectern and started speaking as if everyone should know what he was talking about---BB's mind awoke. It seemed that African art was treated as anthropology or ethnology. The class was actually held in one of the natural history wings and there were many African sculptures jumbled in with geological specimens and stuffed birds. Before BB knew what had hit him, Vogel had turned him on.

Vogel went on with his lecture describing incomprehensible visions of floating downstream into small villages, with lots of hippos, birds and an occasional croc following—it sounded like a scene from a Conrad novel. All of this felt like a new kind of adventure, and BB found himself unexpectedly a captivated student.

He learned about the art world and the money involved and access to big foundations and museum endowments and fellowships that would actually pay people to discover new art. The lectures were packed with fresh information; contentious ideas and Vogel even suggested that the issues of determining provenance were different in Africa than in more developed places.

During the first slide show Vogel showed some classic pictures of fertility goddesses with highly pointed, stylized tits. "Jesus," BB thought to himself, "how the hell could his room mate fall asleep in a class like this. Just look at those tits. Who were these goddesses anyway? What is this *she* replacing the *he* in this new pantheon of Gods?" BB laughed aloud when Vogel told the class how much some of these sculptures were going for in the art market. Nor would he have admitted to anyone his need for breasts. Something in BB ignited when he saw those African women.

Eventually, BB chose the History of Art with a minor in primitivism. He graduated with a M.A. and then went on the fast track to achieve his PhD. Far more than the doctorate, BB saw this as a union ticket into the inner sanctum of the sophisticates. Vogel taught him the refinements not only of his chosen profession amidst the art patrons and academic snobs; but more importantly he learned the practical skills of doing research out in the field---how to identify, date, catalogue. His experience in the merchant marines had also helped Vogel to set up an interview with the famous Henry Seton Chilton.

***

The vast halls of the administration building were awesomely still. The man felt he was inside a maze following endless corridors. It was dark, and most of the employees had gone home. A night guard sat in the reception area. Henry Seton Chilton's office door remained wide open and a beam of light shone out into the corridor. Like a beacon, it led BB forward as he realized this was the map to follow for his interview. He walked towards the light, but halfway down he stopped to smooth his tousled hair and to straighten his tie. BB knew that he was about to meet the head honcho at the Furst Museum at Harvard University and this could take him on the next leg of his career. He also knew that during World War II Set Chilton had been a spy.

Chilton was a Boston Brahmin, and had been a navy man.

He was a known yachtsman and his friends called him "Set." BB knew that Set Chilton epitomized the ideal gentleman in his class. BB could visualize Set Chilton standing next to Jacob Astor when the *Titanic* went down. One could hear a Guggenheim say both to an Astor and to a Chilton: "Tell my wife, I played the game out straight and to the end. No woman shall be left aboard this ship because I was a coward." BB had first observed this code when he worked summer vacations at the yacht clubs. He still wanted into this social stratum.

CHAPTER 3

"HELLO, YOUNG MAN---COME IN, COME in. Glad you could find me this time of evening. It's very rare these days to find me in the office this late, but if Jim Vogel sent you then that's good enough for me. I was just reading something that *Agamemnon* said when he was speaking about Helen of Troy: Want to hear it?" Set Chilton did not wait for an answer.

"Hell to ships, hell to men, hell to cities."

"Being an old seaman, thought you'd like that one. So, let me tell you how I got started...sit down, sit right down and make yourself comfortable. Want a scotch and soda?" Set moved to his bar hidden behind a bookcase and preceded to make the drinks.

"I don't know how much Jim Vogel told you about me—about us--but we hooked up under General William J. Donovan. He was known as "Wild Bill." Vogel was a young chap out of Princeton. I was a navy man, myself. Back then the Navy and the Army had separate code-breaking departments that not only competed, they refused to share any break-through. God-damndest, stupidest organization that I ever heard of. Well, Vogel and I—we changed all that. Can you imagine that son-of-a- bitch—Henry Stimson---he was Secretary of State, doncha'know, and he shut the bastards down because he said that gentlemen don't read each other's mail. Can you imagine that? Ever heard of any spy operation that doesn't read the enemy's mail? So FDR directed Bill Donovan, a World War I veteran, Medal of Honor recipient and New York lawyer, to draft a plan for an intelligence service. Ol' Bill signed me up and that's how I met Vogel---in the beginning we collected and analyzed strategic information required by the Joint Chiefs of Staff and then under Wild Bill's direction, we took off."

"Of course, seeing as how we were both trained it didn't take the higher ups long to figure out where we belonged. We were first posted at Bethesda—actually, it was in a country club, don'cha know, pretty damn good chow, too." At that both BB and Set guffawed. "I can tell you're a seaman if you can laugh about food!"

"Here, let me give you a cigar and you just settle back while I give you my overview of what kind of man we need for these times. I gather you want to join the club? Correct?" Set looked for just a nod and BB gave it being attentive and what a mouth he had on him, laughed BB to himself, I'm not sure what he's talking about in terms of a job—but I'll listen up. I feel as though I'm back in Chelsea and definitely on a ship. This guy is terrific—all this was going through BB's mind as he enjoyed the old coot's conversation…a real character!

BB soon realized that Set was sensing him out and getting the 'cut of his jib' as they said in Set's circles. When suddenly BB realized this man was discussing a covert operation. He was giving this history lesson as only partial information since the old salt had been in the Bureau long enough to know how to discuss a mission without giving away any real information.

"When I was a young fellow—now that was in the final years of WW I---I learned that my family's publishing investments supplied books to American servicemen. They were paid for those books, don'cha know, and that shocked me. That was my first lesson in business because my grandfather said to me, "Everyone is being paid—soldiers, weapon manufacturers, and publishers."

"Yep, I was disillusioned when he told me this because as a young idealist at that time I thought we were 'fighting the war to end all wars' but that's when I found out that the underlying name of the game was making war profiteering money. International crime is really taking over and like the narcotic nightmare; the art plunderers are back at it. This is nothing new. If the world knew how the government collaborated with other governments behind the scenes—well, just look at the Swiss collaboration with the Nazis. They were the fences, no doubt about it, and the reason I know for sure is that Vogel and I were sent over to Zurich by the OSS to head up the "art squad." That's why I quoted Agamemnon—it's throughout history, the art plundering, and more. We need a young and fresh face to cover Africa and that's why Vogel recommended you come to talk with me. Vogel tells me your sharp and with your sea background that you might be a good candidate. We have a hunch that many of the stolen goods are going out of certain ports and onto cargo ships. Interested?"

"Yes, sir," BB answered as if he were saluting. "I am very much interested. It all sounds very mysterious and intriguing."

"Good, good. Now, you see BB, may I call you this?" BB nodded his head in approval. "Good, good...now, as I was saying, it's a whole different ballgame today. The bad guys live off legitimate art dealers and in turn off private collections when they steal the loot. And it's central banks that become the launderers for the deposits. I haven't even mentioned the insurance premiums adding a whole new dimension. The worst parasites and underhanded schemers you'd ever want to know. And most of them," fumed Set, "are members of my own club! No one can figure out the art heist at the Isabella Stewart Gardner Museum. That is baffling all of us. Walked right in the door, they did."

"Scholars, financiers, people in high society—that's how infuriating it is. But I'm getting off the track. BB, I need a man in Africa, with a professional art background, but with judgment and understanding of the realities---and, well, an eye. Do you know that even the IRA got involved? Next thing you know, it will be these goddamned fundamentalists using stolen art as collateral in order to release fanatical jihadists. I mean, just look at those Basques holding the Spanish government to ransom with Velasquez's 'Surrender of Breda' from the Prado." Set was off on another rill. "Yes sir, art theft is still a lucrative business and now we've got a run on all these tin soldiers playing dictators in these developing African countries ---add to this, they're tied up with the diamond trades and who knows what else. Goddamn mess, that's what it is. Besides that, we've got some delicate trade negotiations going on regarding the oil and plutonium and all kinds of natural resources everyone's after. Now, we know some of these offshore companies are more than willing to get more tax deductible benefits if they buy some of the art on the Black Market. Then, they wash it through assorted banking systems. Hell, this has been going on since Malraux. Look what that sonofabitch got away with. Why he practically stole all of Cambodia for the French before he was through. "

"My daughter says none of these profits will go into building schools or hospitals or infrastructures such as bringing clean water and basic needs to the locals. She thinks we ought to be teaching the arts to the indigenous kids so they can get a sense of their roots. She's got a point. Can you imagine those god-damned captured Greeks as they watched Roman wagons loaded down with marble statues and carting them back to pagan Rome?"

This was BB's introduction to Set Chilton. The man was a walking encyclopedia and paced up and down in front of him as he talked a mile a minute. Set was dressed in a Brooks Brothers three-piece suit, proper vest, the whole banking investment look, and his eyes were disturbingly intense and very green. He might look like a Boston Brahmin but he talked like a longshoreman. BB had also done his homework. He had read that Chilton had been decorated with the Navy Cross, amongst other honors, and that he served on some of the most prestigious boards in Boston. He continued to listen with amazement as Set reeled off the titles of some of the seminars BB had taken, the grades he'd received, and detailed information about his dissertation—the man held a whole dossier on him, including his military record.

Chilton pulled out his pipe and started sucking on the chewed up stem and suddenly his face became very serious. Choosing his words carefully, he said: "Okay, BB, if you are interested in developing this conversation, why don't you meet me next Tuesday for lunch at the Harvard Club. In this way, the conversation can continue and we'll have a chance to know one another. The relationship built over the next few weeks; and then one Tuesday, Set stood up after draining his cup of coffee, reached out to shake BB's hand and said, "I trust my gut with you BB. Come to dinner at Louisburg Square on Saturday night and meet my family. I'm having a few houseguests and there's someone I want you to meet. Of course, you do realize that we would have to vet you since this would be a top clearance operation. I think my daughter might be home for the weekend, too. Julia's quite a woman. She's also a very good writer. About your age, I would say. My sister Net runs the house for me since Julia's mother died. Don't be fooled by Net---she's sharp as a tack even though she likes to pretend she's an eccentric old Yankee. Cocktails begin at seven. Net doesn't like her dinner to get cold so she serves at eight o'clock sharp---and the whole thing runs like a clock."

BB rose to shake Chilton's hand again. The deal was practically made. BB was almost inside the door.

CHAPTER 4

LOUISBURG SQUARE IS A PRIVATE square located in the Beacon Hill, Boston, Massachusetts neighborhood. It was named for the 1745 Battle of Louisburg, in which Massachusetts Militiamen sacked the French Fortress located on the site. The elegant houses around the square reflect the rarefied privilege enjoyed by the 19th century upper class in Beacon Hill. *The Atlantic Monthly* editor William Dean Howells, teacher A. Bronson Alcott and his daughter, author Louisa May Alcott, are among the famous people who have lived there in the 19th century. Currently it is the most expensive residential neighborhood in the country and United States Senators' owned townhouses in the prestigious neighborhood.

Set Chilton's family had lived in the square a very long time. His ancestors had been involved with Harrison Gray Otis to purchase land and donate some of it to the State, and that parcel became the famous Boston Capitol whose dome was designed by Charles Bulfinch. They were determined that Boston would remain the capitol, and Otis quietly arranged his Mt. Vernon Properties Committee to purchase 18.5 adjoining acres from the agent of John Singleton Copley, who was at that time living in England. Today, the historic neighborhood runs between Beacon Street, Walnut Street, and Mt. Vernon Street through Louisburg Square to Pinckney Street. It was made spacious, with generous street-side setbacks, and large private gardens for residents. In the historic book of records, Chilton's house was a magnificent example of the Greek Revival townhouse.

BB was brushing a speck off his blazer while rushing up the front stairs and did not see the lady in front of him. Neither one was looking as they literally bumped into each other. Julia was struggling to open the door with an arm full of books and a couple of them were falling out of her hands. BB was approaching the foyer. Apologizing profusely, he bent to catch the books as if they were a football. Julia looked up at the person and when she saw a flash of his blue eyes she felt struck by a bolt of lightening.

Aunt Net came rushing out into the hall, "Julia, for heaven's sake we have other guests arriving any minute and you have to get dressed." Turning to BB she said, "Hello, hello—you must be my brother's new protégé. Welcome to our home. I'm Net Chilton. Now take these books and dump them somewhere in the library. I think you'll find Set in there mixing up martinis." Net Chilton had a schoolteacher manner, and both young people automatically did as they were told. BB fumbling with the books was directed to the library and Julia rushed up the stairs to change, glancing furtively at this guest. "Well, it might turn into an interesting evening after all," she thought as she quickened her pace to do Net's bidding.

BB walked into the library and Set was there talking with a man whose face BB could not quite see. As he struggled with Julia's books, the other guest saw him and said, "Here, let me help you with those." They both found a chair to dump the books into.

"Good evening, BB," said Set, "I am very glad you've arrived before the others. I see you bumped into Julia and her two zillion books," he laughed, "I have never seen such a bookworm in my life. BB let me introduce to you the Honorable Michael Murphy, Member of Parliament in the Dail in Ireland. I was a close friend to Michael's father. You might say we did more than run guns together in those earlier days of "the troubles."

"Remember the first time I brought Julia on one of those trips to Dublin, Michael?"

"Oh, you mean the time she got all caught up in the Tinker question?" They both laughed. With a lilting Irish voice, Michael Murphy said to BB: "I can see that you've already met Ms. Chilton, quite a beauty, she is, too. Reminds me of an Irish thoroughbred, that she does. What Set's referring to was her first trip to Dublin and how she pestered me to get her interviews to do a feature story with those in the know about the Irish Tinkers. Of course, I thought she was wasting her time and told her—'Now, Julia don't you be giv'n them any coppers as they'll just spend it on the drink.' "

"Little did we know, " Set interjected, "that she would win an award for a feature story in a magazine on the history of the Irish Tinkers. She really did her research and wrote a hell'uva expose. Very good, it was."

Michael added, "I told her to go and see a Mr. Tewley who owned some coffeehouses in Dublin, as I knew he'd been working on social service and resettlement issues. A Quaker, he was. Apparently she followed up on my lead and b'gosh he took her down to Galway Bay and introduced her to a Tinker family."

"That's my girl," laughed Set.

"Now, BB, I want you to get together with Michael while he's in Boston because he has a handle on the smuggling operations that come into the Dublin and Irish ports and how they also get into our own Gloucester and New England ports. You'll find it very interesting. But we better join the other guests or Net will be at me. Come, gentlemen, let us join the ladies."

What BB saw as he entered the living room was a beautifully appointed salon filled with antiques and what looked to him like original paintings on the walls. But what really caught his eye was the woman he had bumped into on the front steps. She was a knockout. A natural beauty with extremely thick brunette hair and the greenest eyes he had ever seen. Just like her father. She quite took his breath away. And, her figure—she looked like a Grecian goddess. She could have been a pinup in one of the lockers on a ship. But this was no bimbo from Chelsea. She wore lustrous and obviously real pearls in her ears and the simple white cotton sundress she was wearing was striking against her tanned and glistening body that oozed health and wellness. BB wanted to reach out and touch her skin. She exuded such a natural sexiness.

People, especially women, came and went in BB's life. He certainly had his share while in the merchant marines. Yet, he knew by instinct that this woman standing before him and speaking to Michael Murphy with her fantastic smile and poised stature was one in a million. No one could take her for granted. In fact, she seemed to BB a bit intimidating even to him because she was so obviously self-assured and put forth such an aristocratic composure of natural grace. Clearly, she had been trained how to be a hostess with her aura of friendliness, brightness and refinement. It wasn't just her finely chiseled face, either, but her whole bearing. A Bostonian and a patrician, she did not appear to be haughty, rather, a woman comfortable in her own body and environment. As the cocktail hour drew to its close, Net announced that dinner was served and when the fifteen guests entered the dining room she said they would fine placement cards around the mahogany table. It was a rich patina of mahogany elegantly set with bone china and heavy silverware settings. Why was BB not surprised to find that he had been seated next to Michael Murphy with Julia Seton Chilton across the table? During the three-course dinner she could converse with them easily. Set was at one end and Aunt Net at the other and around the table were seated a book publisher, a famous heart surgeon, a lawyer that BB had seen on television somewhere and several guests who were colleagues in Set's museum. BB knew that he had been welcomed inside the inner sanctum. He had made it across the Mystic River into the heart of Louisburg Square.

"Tell me William," Michael asked as the lobster bisque was being served. "Have you done any horse racing? I am a director of the Irish Sweepstakes and that's why I am now in Boston. I'm meeting with a couple of people involved in racing at Suffolk Downs. I gather this area might be opening up to casino gambling."

"Interesting," BB responded. "When I was a kid I used to go to the track quite a lot and, in fact, made some money. If you want any contacts, I have a few in Chelsea, Mass." Michael's eyes widened, "No kidding! Has anyone told you about the Irish Sweepstakes?"

"Actually, no. But I would be interested in knowing." BB turned his attention to Michael although he was having a hard time taking his eyes off Julia, and really wanted to engage her in conversation. But she was busily talking to the heart surgeon seated next to her.

"It was a very ingenious idea," said Michael, "and my father and Set had something to do with its startup. I mean, what's a young government to do when faced with the need to build a national health system and limited resources to do it? Well, if you remember "the troubles" the Republic of Ireland had a heck of a time getting started and if it weren't for our Boston friends, I'm not sure we would've made it. So my father got it into his head to raise money to build Irish hospitals and they established the long-distance gambling event that began as the Irish Sweepstakes—and it became the event that took advantage of the love of the Irish around the world for a good horse race. It was held four times a year. Set's family was part of the original investors and, of course, he knew plenty of people on this side of the pond. Gambling was generally illegal so the tickets were marketed internationally and even sold on the black market, reaping considerable funds for the hospital program. Now I know a fellow by the name of Vitori here in Greater Boston who is highly invested in the whole casino development going on. We have some racing ties."

"Excuse me," interrupted BB, "You don't mean Sal Vitori, do you?"

"Why, the very one. Do you know this chap?"

"Know him, he's practically the boy next door. I grew up with his family...many of whom were fishermen out of the port of Gloucester. Set certainly has a lot of connections. It boggles my mind."

At that moment, the lawyer sitting on the other side of Michael asked him a question, so BB turned his attention back to Julia, who was finishing her bisque.

They looked across the table at one another and both of them knew. Definitely, they were going to connect. BB asked the first question.

"Do you sail?"

"Oh, of course. One cannot grow up a Chilton and not sail," she laughed.

"Would you like to go for a sail on Saturday? I have a friend who keeps a small ketch down at the harbor, and whenever I'm in Boston he wants me to use it. Being an old sailor, myself, he trusts me. Perhaps we could have an afternoon sail together?"

"I would enjoy that very much. What time?"

CHAPTER 5

WHEN HE FINALLY LEFT LOUISBURG Square, BB's head was swimming. Everything was moving incredibly fast, and he was as giddy as a teenager about meeting Julia. He had to call Geno right away and find out what was going on with the horseracing scene and to make sure he could use the boat for Saturday. He couldn't believe his luck nor could he figure out the incredible coincidence of Michael Murphy knowing Sal Vitori. Was there no contact that Set did not have? "I wonder," BB thought to himself, "what am I getting into with all of these connections? Well, I'll call Geno and see what he knows."

Geno was still up and glad to hear from BB. The first thing he said was how sorry he was to hear about the deaths earlier in the year of BB's parents. "Odd, isn't it, that Helen didn't last long after Will passed? Funny how that often works." After once again expressing his condolences they chatted about the business and Geno reminded him of something that they had talked about a long time ago. He said, "I've heard about the

Chilton family…you finally hit the big leagues, kid. But there's one thing I want to remind you of, and that's the very long relationship between the Irish, the Boston Brahmins and my own people. Never poke too deeply into their business affairs because you don't know what will come up. That's how I have survived and made it. My family has been good to me and I never ask too many questions about the money and where it originally came from. I would give you the very same advice as you move into this league. And, you know that of course you can use the boat."

"Where do I take a lady to lunch or dinner around here these days?" "You want the best?" asked Geno. "Of course, I want the best. In fact, you can loan me some of that money I've been saving with you." "Well, my friend, that is something we definitely have to talk about over supper. Have you any idea what you've earned? We have to re-invest it somehow, and I have a couple of ideas. So take your gorgeous high-class lady to The Four Seasons, and then meet me the following night for a beer and some clams at Jake's? OK? I gotta' go now, BB, you caught me in the middle of something here." BB laughed as he heard a woman's voice in the background.

On Saturday as they had planned Julia met BB at the dock in the forenoon. "So I take it that you are a good sailor?" Julia asked. "Yes, ma'am, and I also know how to run a launch. Jump in." Julia watched BB closely as he neatly pulled away from the dock. She noticed that the wrinkles around his blue eyes were used to squinting across open water. He had the trim figure and easy agility of an outdoorsman. His eyes were also very penetrating and they looked directly at Julia as if she were a fine piece of art—his eyes almost bore a hole through her; but it was not a lecherous look, yet, it definitely was a man looking at a woman. She felt like a

Maggie on a hot tin roof and she knew almost immediately that she wanted this man to touch her as much as it appeared he wanted to do so. But she was Set Chilton's daughter, and this was a first date. BB certainly did not want to blow it. So he played it cool all afternoon.

Julia handled the jib like an old salt and soon they were tacking out of Boston harbor and sailing close-hauled with the wind forward of the beam on a true reach. They both were a bit tentative as he handed her a cup of coffee and a muffin that he'd picked up at Dunkin' Donuts. "I guess that I ought to warn you that I tend to bark out orders when sailing on a boat. It's the old merchant marine training in me."

"That's perfectly okay," Julia responded. "I learned how to be Set's first mate as a kid and I'm quite used to it. But, I might jump ship if you become too much of a Captain Bly," she chuckled. BB believed it. He knew that he was talking with a strong-minded and independent woman.

"So, tell me, what are you working on? Your father tells me that you are a writer and in the publishing business? You certainly had enough books to sink a ship the other night. A new writing project?"

"Indeed," said Julia. "I'm researching a book on third world women and their educational needs. I am also an editor for my family's publishing company and we publish a lot of art history textbooks."

As the sail got underway, they both began to relax and enjoy the common bond they had in the sea and in art history, so the conversation was very easy. It was a wonderful afternoon and they were in sync with nautical terminology for when he had to sheet in the main she knew exactly what to do and how to take over and handle the tiller like an expert. They were a good team and she could handle the jib and come about exactly

Mamy Wata

on his directive. As they reached the mooring and took the sails down, Julia said, "Thank you for a lovely afternoon. I did not realize that I'd been working so hard. I think this is the first time that I've relaxed in a long time."

"I hope it won't be the last time with me," BB boldly stated. "I would really like to know you, Julia, could you join me for dinner this evening?"

"Yes," she answered him very directly. BB realized then and there that she also was a woman who knew what she wanted. There would be no bullshit in this relationship. The summer turned out to be a beautiful one and Julia and BB had many more sails. She realized as they moved into the dog days of summer that they were courting. BB had, of course, kissed her gently but he never made any untoward advances. She took him up to the island of Vinalhaven off Rockland, Maine to spend a long weekend with Aunt Net at her summer cottage. Net's summerhouse was located next to a quarry and the rock had been used in a variety of buildings, including St. John the Divine in New York City. Vinalhaven was the farthest island out on the edge of the continental shelf and they had to get there via ferry. Vinalhaven was the summer place where Julia had grown up and it was a favorite getaway where she could paint and read at her leisure. She was eager to show it to BB. They also visited the Boston museums and rode on the swan boats and took long rides up the coast eating lobster in the ruff or stopping for a bowl of steamers or some fried clams. They talked about their respective work and their dreams and aspirations. This was the stage when BB told her about Africa, and how he would be collaborating with her father on a project to catalogue African art. He did not tell her that he would be a member of the art squad since this would be a security breach, even if she were Set Chilton's daughter. Increasingly, day-by-day, they found themselves deeply immersed in one another. Still, BB had yet to take the ultimate intimacy step. He knew that this was the woman he wanted to marry and by the end of the summer she knew it, too. Julia and BB fell in love, and it was to change their lives forever.

CHAPTER 6

GENO WAS WAITING FOR BB at Jake's. It was a local joint and known for its great seafood. Geno was nursing a Sam Adams when BB found him at the back of the restaurant.

"Hey, bro'...you look great!"

"So do you, my man. In fact, you are looking mighty prosperous!"

"It's this brew, man. I'm getting a paunch and don't work out like we used to. But I'm busy as hell. That investment we started has raked us in a lot of dough. We need to discuss what you want me to do with your share. The amount you put in was start up-seed money, but it paid off, man. You've got yourself a sizeable stake."

"What do you mean by sizeable? You can tell me about it later; but that's not why I'm here, Geno. I need to ask you to do a little investigating for me. Do you stay in touch with Sal?"

"Of course, we're family. But we don't mix up our businesses. Like I told you a long time ago, BB, when it comes to the family's businesses I keep my mouth shut but my eyes and ears open. As for me, I have a completely prosperous business---I am doing what I love, and I'm making money at it. Hell, I've even moved to one of the old warehouses that they've converted to condos. It's over in East Boston and I have a panoramic view of the harbor. I want you to come for dinner and I'll make you some sauce just like Ma used to make."

"You're on. I'd like to bring someone with me. In fact she's not just someone, but the one. I'm in love, Geno. And I want you to help me find a diamond and be my best man. Does your cousin still run that diamond-clearing house on the South Shore? I want a really fine ring for a very classy woman. Not ostentatious, mind you, but something that's, well, top of the line."

"Yes, he does and I'll take you down there. I'm honored that you want me to be your best man, and you know that I will. So, tell me what's she like? God dammit, man, we have so much to talk about I don't know where to start."

"First things first. Let's order. I am craving some of Jake's fried clams, and then I want to hear about your business, and more. I guess you are a big man in the racing world…right?"

The waiter came to order and Geno asked for a couple of more beers.

"Man, you would not believe it. I own the largest subsidiary of BMW motorcycles in all of New England. I also sponsor and own a racing team at NASCAR so I spend a lot of my time now down at Daytona Beach where I have a condo. Very slick place. The whole nine yards—pool, tennis, and restaurant— you name it. Did you know that BMW was originally an aircraft manufacturer at the turn of the century? The company was very big in Germany and throughout World War I when they introduced their first motorcycle under the name, the R32. That was in 1923, but with the Armistice, at the Treaty of

Versailles, the German air force was banned so they diversified and eventually went into manufacturing the R32 under the BMW product line. They've been world wide ever since and the R32 became the foundation for all future motorcycles. During World War II, BMW motorcycles performed exceptionally well in the harsh environment of the North African deserts. At the beginning of the war, the German army needed as many vehicles as it could get of all types. In the desert, the protruding cylinders of the flat-twin engine and shaft drive performed better than vertical and V-twin engines, which overheated in the hot air, and chain drives were fucked up by desert sand. Well, as you can imagine, at the end of the war BMW, like the rest of Germany, was in ruins and all their plants outside of Munich were destroyed by allied bombings. The Soviets took what was left as reparations and dismantled what was left of the machines and sent them all back to the Soviet Union where they were reassembled to make Ural motorcycles. Anyhow, to make a long story short, when the ban on production was lifted in allied controlled West Germany, BMW had to start from scratch. There were no plans, blueprints, or schematic drawings, so they had to go on the old plans of R32 and then they came up with a newer model, the 250 cc R24. As things progressed other competitors went out of business and by 1957 BMW exported 85% of its twin-powered motorcycles to the United States. And that was when my love affair with engines began. Obviously, the state of the art has expanded and I got into the game at just the right time. So, my man, that's where your initial investment is. BB, we're rich, for Christ's sake. While you've been sailing the seven seas and farting around with African tits, I have managed to take our little nest egg and turn it into the golden egg."

"Geno, I'm really proud of you. But I don't have one iota of what to tell you about my share. Why don't you just keep it moving for my retirement? I'm not really into making a lot of money, Geno. What I've been looking for is, well, status in my field of choice, and adventure. And, I've found it. So keep on earning with my share, okay? But take a chunk out so we can buy a diamond for Julia."

"Brother, I think we ought to invest some of your money in a racing car team. NASCAR is big…and I mean big. You can still remain a silent partner and I'll handle all the business angles. And when you're ready, you can retire, man, and buy your schooner and sail the seven seas. How does that sound?"

"Sounds terrific. But right now I want to talk with you about horse racing. Specifically about this guy from Ireland who's meeting Sal—it has something to do with horse racing and casino gambling. Can you find out anything?"

"Listen, my friend. I have protected you all of my life from things you did not need to know. But I think it is time that you get a deeper picture. First of all, you need to know that your father-in-law-to-be is not all that lily white."

"Geno, I know that he was in the OSS during World War II, is that what you're getting at?"

"Let me give you some background information from the family's perspective. You know, BB, we all kinda' protected you to go and do your thing—and it was different, that's for sure. Who the hell would've thought you'd end up looking at African tits, for Chris' sake."

They both laughed as Geno continued to share what he knew with BB: "There's a lot of history between us Sicilians, the Boston Irish, and the Boston Brahmins. In terms of your future father-in-law, well, no one really seems to know if he's been legit all of these years. Everyone knows that he was with the OSS, but whether he was (and still is) an informer with the FBI or if he's had some kind of a cut on the deals that have gone down---well, honestly, I don't know."

"To understand this whole thing, we have to go back to Ireland and this might be why Michael Murphy is talking with Sal. Still, I have no idea what Sal is up to, but I do know that the Irish connect somehow with the powers that be on Beacon Hill—and everyone knows that the Chilton family has been a powerbroker since the beginning of the Commonwealth. I do know that the Irish from Southie, and the Sicilians from the North End connect together; and I guess it is part of the mythology as to the role that these people played and continue to play when deals go down. Certainly, they ran guns to support the Feinians in helping the Irish to ultimately gain their independence. I know that these guys started an Irish International Bank in Dublin and that Set Chilton is on the board along with Mike Murphy. Still, it seems that the problems in Northern Ireland with the British never seem to end."

"I also know that the FBI was trying to infiltrate La Cosa Nostra and break into all the so-called gangs. Their territories were clearly bounded—the Mafia held forth in the North End, East Boston, Revere, Chelsea, the North Shore. The Irish gang controlled South Boston, the South End, Charlestown, Dorchester, Somerville and the South Shore. The question remains, where did the Boston Brahmins fit in? Maybe they were a conduit between the two factions and the politics up on the hill. I really can't say, and I'm not sure that anyone outside the inner-sanctum knows. Nobody talks and it's a very tightly controlled organization. Even as a member of the family, I know very little. Only what I've heard around the margins, so to speak."

"What I do suspect, though, and this is just between you and me, buddy, is that all the talk about bringing casinos into the State makes me wonder what type of deals might now be going down. I know that my family has been heavily involved in gambling over the years. Whether or not Sal is somehow tied into all of this I do not know. Besides, he wouldn't tell me if he was, and if he did tell me and I said anything outside of the family, well...you know. I suggest that you keep this conversation between the two of us. In terms of this Mike Murphy from Ireland visiting Sal---if I had to guess—or bet—I would think it might have more to do with the casino operations. I am sure everyone wants a piece of that. You know that my Uncle Nino is a very big power in the Massachusetts legislature?" BB nodded his head in the negative. "Sure. He was born and raised on Prince Street—you know, Prince Spaghetti Day? And when election time comes around, so does Nino. I don't know what more to tell you, except that we've always had a lot of aficionados in the North End involved at the track. I can see that they would all want some gambling closer to home. Casinos seem to be the new thing—and maybe they do raise money for the State, just like the Irish Sweepstakes did for Ireland. Nino represents the North End and parts of Beacon Hill near the State House, where the Chilton's live—and Set most certainly is involved in the Financial District, which Nino also covers. So, why this guy Murphy is visiting Set and what does it all mean? I don't know if I'll ever have the whole picture. It's an interesting puzzle. The long and short of it, BB, is to keep your own nose clean, your eyes open, and play the cards close to your chest. That's what I've had to do. Maybe a whole new chapter is opening up in your life, who knows?"

"I hear you, brother. I may very well be sailing into uncharted waters."

"In that case, buddy, my advice is to keep your life jacket nearby, and call me if you need any help. Now, tell me about Julia. I can't wait to meet her."

Chapter 7

Set and Net could see what was happening and Set told his sister that he approved of the relationship. "Julia would never be happy with just another Boston Brahmin. BB is a man and he'll bring new blood into this family. Besides, if she is half as in love with him as I was with her mother, she'll be a happy woman." When in August they announced that they wanted to get married before leaving for Africa, Set gave them his blessing.

It was a small family wedding in the Church of the Advent on Brimmer Street, just down the hill from the house. Geno came and stood with his buddy. Aunt Net stood with Julia. The basilica shaped sanctuary at the church was dignified and the ceremony simple. Following the service, they all went to the Ritz for a luncheon. Julia and BB were flying out that evening for Africa. This trip was a honeymoon gift from Set for he wanted them to see as much as possible of Africa before settling in at Owerri on the west coast of the Continent.

"I want you kids to see where man was born and wild grasses blow forever. You need to read Peter Matthison who wrote about all of this. He said, and I can quote him, something such as "the silhouette almost lost to us all in this age of modernity is that of the African man of silence standing in the distance—his spear point glistening in the sun. He is tall and gaunt and black with scars and raised beads of skin from temple to temple."

"This is the old Africa. This is what you must seek out before you get caught up in the incredible complexities of a third world country desperately trying to come into a first world era of globalization."

"Just think of it, Julia," said Set who glided into his romantic view: "old millenniums during the Pleistocene and after, the ancient rivers of the Ice Age; wind spun sands, fossil tracings in the sands of the Sahara. Picture the hunters once wandering there, leaving red drawings on rocks. A very long time ago, Julia, when Asia brought wheat and barley, sheep and goats, to the lower Nile, and the desert was already spreading, and the work of those droughts was already advancing. Then, by 3500 BC, domestic stock appeared by way of the Mediterranean and the opening up of the great north-south caravan routes across the desert. This is what I want you to feel as you sleep under a mosquito net in a camp." As always, Set was caught up in his imagination of history as they prepared to leave and say goodbye.

And so after Set had a private business meeting with BB, the newlyweds set forth on their great adventure and on really knowing one another. Their lovemaking was beyond what Julia might have imagined. BB was gentle and moved in slow motion, but strong. She had never really known or understood the power of her body until BB awakened her. BB had an animal magnetism and he knew how to arouse her and make her moan with longing. His tongue licked her, inch by inch, and when he finally entered what he called her mound of Venus, it set her whole body on fire. They looked into one another's eyes and could see the pleasure. When, the first time he took her buttocks in his hands, lifting her whole pelvis, plunging his erect penis so deeply, so hard, she gasped; but soon, she learned how to keep pace with his rhythm, sometimes languorously slow, sometimes hot and fast, and when he came, she thought he would consume her flesh as she reached for her own orgasm. They slept. They dreamed. They awoke in the wonder of one another and when she had her first multiple orgasms it was as if a field of electricity surrounded them.

Other nights the time passed slowly, floating as if in a dreamlike state, in a cocoon of their mosquito netting as they listened to distant drums and sounds of wild creatures in the night. They were nourished by one another and by the exotic world surrounding them. When he was deep within her, she licked his eyes, sucked juices from his mouth as if she was a Queen bee transferring her honey into his body, making him feel even stronger. He wanted her more. He always wanted her. He was almost stunned that he could love this woman so passionately—suckling her breasts, stroking her hair, twining his large hands in hers, drawing his fingers across her high cheekbones with infinite tenderness. They drifted, danced, and caught themselves in the sexual tension then the still point after their physical awakening. It was as if they were suspended in some ancient time with no past or future. They would bathe together with aloe and coconut scents and become aware of one another's clues. She loved to look, and touch his erect penis ready to take her again—to move together as she helped to direct his hardness into her. Then, as the drums pounded— their bodily scents mingling together of earth smells--they would offer one another to the bliss of what seemed to act as sharing and receiving seeds from a pomegranate.

They watched as an Arab dhow sailed into Zanzibar and during the weeks that followed, they saw elephants crossing the plain below Kilimanjaro, and a million pink flamingoes, and tribes of people with incredible colors and patterns in their clothing wearing striking beaded jewelry. The expectations that Set wanted for the couple came true on their idyllic honeymoon. Julia was awakening each day to the mysteries of Africa and the deeper knowing of the man she had married.

***

They had started the honeymoon in North Africa--in Morocco—and it was there that Julia and BB were introduced and hosted by Charles Chantel, who was Dominique's brother. He was quite a character, and it turned out that Charles had inherited the family's import-export business. He had set Dominique up with enough capital for her art gallery businesses to flourish. The family villa had been turned into a museum after their parents had died. Charles lived somewhat modestly in a suite of apartments in his family's old villa overlooking a well-known Marrakech Square. Charles said that he traveled so much that it didn't make sense for him to keep up a large place, so it worked better for him to have a latchkey residence. He also had a place in Rome overlooking the Spanish Steps.

Dominique's brother was a very charismatic person. Amongst his other enterprises he was also a film producer doing documentaries and when Julia and BB arrived in Marrakech, Charles was preparing to go on a film shoot for the king of Morocco. He was about to do a documentary for the tourist board. "Come with me, and I'll show you the real country. We'll drive over the High Atlas Mountains to Agadir and then I'll take you on to Casablanca where you can get a flight down to Africa proper. I do want to come and visit you in Owerri because my work takes me almost everywhere. What's interesting about Agadir," Charles went on, "is that it's a city that was destroyed by an earthquake and it was completely rebuilt with the new architecture and a planned community blending the old Moorish with modern amenities right on the edge of the Sahara." BB and Julia jumped at the opportunity to see this through Charles' eyes.

First, Charles gave them a tour of Marrakech. "It's called the "Pearl of the South" or "The Rose City" – these are just a few of the nicknames this desert city has acquired over the years. The pearl and the jewel symbolize Marrakech's importance as the center of Morocco ever since it was a trading and resting place on the crossroads of ancient caravan routes from Timbuktu. The rose attests to a city still painted entirely in salmon pink, in keeping with the red-clay earth below."

"This is a city virtually unchanged since the Middle Ages, and its ramparts encircle and protect its mysterious labyrinthine markets, or medina, which hide palaces and the ornate mansions of wealthy merchants, and some of the most colorful bazaars in the Arab world. We're at the foot of the snowcapped High Atlas Mountains and this city has been stubbornly defended against marauding tribes by successive Berbers and other powerful dynasties. The Spaniards built the underground irrigation system; but it was the French and Winston Churchill's influence as European stakeholders collaborated with DeGaulle and the spoils of war that kept a tight colonial control until it became an independent monarchy. As the Marrakshis say, "Insh' Allah" (God willing)—what will be, will be. We have two distinct parts: the walled-in medina, or the Old City, and the wide-open New City, or Ville Nouvelle. We have a labyrinth of narrow alleys in which our houses, the souks, and the bazaars form an interlocking honeycomb, specifically designed to confuse invaders. The famous Djemaa el Fna Square is the heartbeat of Marrakech, whose name translates roughly as "Meeting Place at the End of the World." Today, a circumferential highway that was built by the French surrounds the open area. Between the two large archways there is a huge park and a fun fair ground and I'll show you the very large market area where anything can be bought and sold. If you want some good hashish, BB, this is the place. I will show you where Dominique has a gallery and next-door is an excellent collection of Moroccan antique crafts that include all kinds of leatherwork and pottery and other artifacts. Next to the museum is a beautiful mosque. The old palace courtyard is stunning and filled with flowers and cypress trees and furnished with a gazebo and fountain; and the adjacent salons burst with more jewelry and diamond shops, daggers, and ornate kaftans. Here we will have dinner overlooking roof terraces that will give you a panoramic view of the open-air entertainment that always mesmerizes the crowds; cobra charmers with raucous flutes, wild acrobats, dancers, and musicians with clashing cymbals; and a mélange of monkey tamers, fortune-tellers, henna ladies, tooth pullers, and astrologers, you name it."

"The best time to behold all of this is at sunset, when the whole square turns purple, orange, or deep pink and it takes on its smoky nighttime glow from the hundreds of gas lamps that light the still-sizzling food stalls. This is where most of the Marrakshis come out to meet, eat, and be entertained. So we'll have a siesta and drinks and then head out the door."

It was, indeed, quite a remarkable evening and after spending the night in Marrakesh, they got up early to pack and piled into Charle's red Volkswagen bus with camera equipment hanging from the luggage rack. Julia jumped in front and BB started a conversation with Charles's two cameramen, as the men climbed into the back of the bus. They even had a police escort provided by the king, himself. "Never know about bandits up in the mountainous regions, and the passes can get a bit tricky as we climb in altitude. Besides, the king is paying for this whole shoot-- so what the hell---we might as well go first class. Wait until I show you where our accommodations will be tonight."

At the top of Africa, the High Atlas Mountain range rises like a wall, a natural fortress between the fertile Haouz plain around Marrakesh and the deserts of the South. "They often have been called the Forbidden Atlas,'" said Charles, as they made their way up the rugged road surrounded by a wild region of intransigent tribesmen and powerful local feudal lords. "Boasting a series of peaks over 13,000 feet, much of the moisture blows in from the Atlantic, and the mountains return some of it to the farmers of the northern Moroccan plains and send some out in thin rivers that vanish into the desert."

"But there are limits to the number of people even this intensive agriculture can support, so the Berbers can be found along the roads. As you can see, the sheer peaks, the tumbling gorges are strikingly etched into the sides of the mountain villages and the way these people still live offer incredible contrasts with modernity, and it is all a scene that goes back to biblical times. Here you will find the genes of invading Vandals, Greek settlers, Roman bureaucrats, Phoenician sailors, and Arab scholars along with those of sub-Saharan soldiers, gold miners, and salt traders. This is a remarkable panoply of history," said Charles, who was, indeed, a great travel guide and knew so much of the history and its culture.

"Even Winston Churchill stayed at the oasis I will take you to tonight. He used to come here to paint and take the cures. It is the most exclusive resort in all of Morocco, the Gazelle d'Or – "the golden gazelle." As you will soon see, it offers secluded bungalows with shaded but airy wooden shutters and exquisitely tastefully decorated rooms. They are furnished with the best of the Moroccan, French and British décor. Each one of the bungalows has its own private terrace surrounded by jasmine and orange blossoms—this is truly an oasis on the edge of the Sahara—and you will see why it was a favorite of Churchill. All of the bungalows are arranged around irrigated watered lawns and an excellent pool, believe it or not, beside the Sahara. You will also taste the finest cuisine in this country."

As they climbed higher and higher up the High Atlas range the scenery changed and the road got narrower. Along the side of the road they could see shepherds tending their flocks all wearing the classic dejallah with a hood to keep the sand and dust off. All of a sudden they rounded a curve and the road was impassable. A rockslide. BB and the camera crew got out to start moving the rocks. The policeman went up the road to a local village to get help from some locals. During the wait, Julia had time to ask Charles about their parents.

"I've been wanting a chance to ask you what you know about our fathers and how they met during World War II. You were so much older than Dominique and me, do you have any memories of them?" asked Julia.

"You know that the French and the British put them together?" Charles asked. "It's quite a fascinating story, really. My Dad was with the French Resistance and they were investigating some stolen gold and other art artifacts that were being looted by the Nazis. In early 1943, I think it was FDR who established the American Commission for the Protection and Salvage of Artistic and Historical Monuments in the War Areas. It was called The Roberts Commission. They proposed that men already enlisted in the armed forces that were "qualified" museum officials and art historians…could be attached to this operation in the European theater. I believe around that time the Chairman of the Commission, who was a Justice Roberts, hence the name, met with William J. Donovan, director of OSS, requesting that a special intelligence unit deal with the looted art and stolen gold. They wanted a Frenchman, and that is why my Dad was chosen. It was in this operation that our fathers met. Donovan agreed because he also thought that certain Nazi agents could be using art looting and collaborative activities to conceal their roles as espionage agents. Furthermore, it is my understanding from what my father told me, that the selected members were interested in tracing the flow of assets to places of refuge where they might be used to finance the postwar survival of Nazism. So they were dealing with a lot of crooks."

"Our fathers were considered 'hunters' of Nazi art and other assets?" Julia asked. "I am completely intrigued because my father never talked about his war experiences with me."

"Well, I was told that naval officers were chosen from the United States and my Dad was chosen because, you know, he also spoke fluent German. Did you know that he had married a Krupp from the famous German industrial family? She was not my mother as they were divorced in the late 20's but my father married and then had annulled several marriages he had made with Jewesses, and that's how he got a few of his friends out of Germany. He had incredible access due to the fact that he was integrally involved with that family. But, he had by then also joined the Resistance and both of our fathers had more freedom of movement than others in the military, not only due to their fine-arts backgrounds—my father had already inherited our import-export business from my Moroccan grandfather—but both of our parents were somehow involved in the investigation and interrogation of Nazis and Germans involved in these confiscations. I think there were repositories for the loot all over the place—including Africa. Allied forces also discovered mines and caves where the Third Reich moved things into a centralized storage area in Switzerland. Despite their tireless efforts, however, hundreds of confiscated art works and gold bars were never recovered or returned to their rightful owners. And, to this day, it is an open question. It is believed that tons of the gold still remains to be recovered."

"Do you think that my father has an idea about this gold and where it ended up?" Julia asked.

"I think you would have to ask your father, Julia. It has been suggested that he knows more than he ever let on; but it is also said that he kept quiet not only for his own safety but because he continued to be involved with the CIA once the OSS folded into that agency after the war."

"I never knew any of this," said Julia. "My dad has certainly protected me over all these years. But this gives me a lot of food for thought. When I see him again, I will try to talk with him about that time of his life. Thank you for sharing this with me, Charles."

Just then they could see a group of people walking up the path with dust swirling around them. It was the men and behind them a group of young lads who soon were able to remove the rocks so that they could pass. The troupe finally continued down the other side of the High Atlas and just as Charles promised, around sunset they drove through an arch of orange and jasmine trees arriving at what could only be described as a piece of Eden on earth. Everything that Charles had promised them about the Gazelle d'Or took them into a Scheherazade experience. Satiated with the best of French wines and food and an evening of stimulating conversation mostly with European guests staying at the oasis, they fell into a trance of sophisticated living and finally retired to pack up for the morning trip that was to take them to the edge of the Sahara desert to Agadir.

Charles said that many Moroccans thought of Agadir as not really being Moroccan and not really European; It seems placeless," he said. "The earthquake destroyed the place, so the whole thing was rebuilt after the rubble was razed and today it is a brand new, modern city where even Moroccans feel fewer social restraints than in other towns and cities."

"Why, all the buildings are white," exclaimed BB, as they drove into Agadir.

"Yes. Quite an effect, is it not? A few miles down the road is an old friend of mine. He has built his very own medina. Each stone in his village is laid by hand. The decorations follow both Berber and Saharan motifs. You should be able to get some fine things for your new home in Owerri and I am sure that they could be shipped, Julia." Julia did, in fact, order some beautiful Moroccan tables and other artifacts and Charle's friend said he would ship them to Owerri.

It turned out to be a spectacular visit with Charles and they were quite exhausted when Charles finally brought them to Casablanca where they said their farewells and were boarded onto the flight South.

Avoiding the hot spots of war in this huge continent, they went first to safari country; then, onward up the western coast on the Atlantic Ocean side. They took their time and stayed in game parks and watched the animals come to drink at the water holes as they sat on a shaded verandah and sipped a cool drink. They watched as women passed along their paths bearing cargoes on their heads, swaying like cobras through the blowing grasslands, laughing with a band of girls, straight-backed, high breasted, flirting and waving. They saw men painting gray ash or red ocher on their bodies to celebrate a special day or ritual. One morning they watched two naked fishers, laughing and arguing, handling a casting net, while exotic birds flitted through the reeds. Julia shivered as the river danced, "For a moment," she said to BB, "I feel a sudden sadness as if it is not real and will not last---there is such a primeval splendor and rawness in it. In Owerri, I want to know the people. I don't want to live like a segregated colonialist...do you?"

That night they watched the golden colors of the savannah, and in that strange light they saw a cheetah slip across a track. All of these scenes and experiences enhanced their own animal instincts, as they got lost in each other's arms. "Yes, we have a lot to learn here, my beauty," as he wrapped her in his arms." Let's leave it all to another day and to our future and live in the present for now. You know, I don't question what is as much as you do, Julia. My job, you know, might be such that I have to kow-tow to some of the so-called "colonialists" and we are in a vast place, you know. We know there is a huge dark side here. We have a history going back to the slave trade and the Boers and the diamond exploitations, and King Leopold and the rubber---so much more."

"Yes, agreed Julia, "there is so much to learn and what I've read thus far about that creep Cecil Rhodes and his DeBeers Company makes me want to puke."

BB laughed and said, "The diamond on your finger probably came from that company. After all, he did give the world the Rhodes Scholarships. Economics is economics, Julia. Always has been and always will be."

"Now, you sound just like my father. What is it that you two are up to here, anyway?"

But BB did not answer her. "It's true that the nations of Europe carved this place up—British, Germans, Belgians, Dutch, French, Portuguese—then the cold war and now the new terrorism and tribalism." We can't solve the world's problems, and certainly the issues on this Continent are overwhelming, Julia. We will do the best that we can in Owerri. But let's not get too serious yet." He reached for her, and their lovemaking began again.

CHAPTER 8

OWERRI IS LOCATED IN WEST Africa and it's about the size of California, and just as diverse. People said that Owerri represented all of Africa in one region. It also contained much cultural diversity as the British, Germans and the French had all at sometime or another occupied the country. Its broad geography included plains as well as mountain regions, desert and jungle, cities and villages and seaside towns. The scenery as Julia had read was said to be exceptional and the indigenous people hailed from many different parts of the Continent; thus making up such a vast array of differences. Christianity makes up 40% of Owerri's religious beliefs and 40% are Islamic, while 20% hold onto traditional beliefs.

The house that Set had arranged for them by his intermediaries stood in a shaded enclave with a view of the Atlantic at the edge of the coast. A small botanical garden enclosed them within a surrounding and well-screened veranda where Eucalyptus trees, Frangipani shrubs, Flame trees,

Poinsettias, Flowering Hibiscus, and other exotic flora and fauna emitted a perfumed and tropical aroma. The main house was situated in the compound with two smaller buildings for the staff and a smaller one for storage. The house was built from adobe and the roof was made of red tiles. The inside ceilings exposed the wooden beams that supported the whole edifice. The walls were all in a whitewashed plaster with a number of windows looking out on the veranda. Banana and pine trees surrounded the back of the encircling veranda and provided welcoming shade.

Julia fell in love with the house as soon as she saw it. She placed her writing desk on the veranda so she could see the waves roll into shore. BB quickly took possession of the good-sized storage cabin, which he immediately made into his office. A housekeeper and a cook had been provided. Set had seen to it all via an agent. Chisale and Mutanda are a married couple and Chisale fast became a good companion to Julia. Mutanda was BB's guide and went with him when out on a field trip. This left Chisale to help Julia orientate herself to the village and to many parts of Owerri. Julia loved the furniture in the main house that was mostly made out of wicker and woven substances that looked like jute and bamboo. The other pieces had been carefully chosen and were made of local hard woods. Julia could not have chosen better if she had decorated it herself. The accoutrements that they had bought on their trip in Morocco with Charles had arrived and inside were oriental rugs, tooled leather hassocks and a large brass coffee table. She also chose some local Batik cloth to upholster the chairs and couch and they contrasted with the whitewashed walls on which they hung African sculpture and African masks and other Primitive art pieces that BB had started collecting. The whole bungalow was very comfortable and quite dramatic. The centerpiece of the living room was a large fieldstone fireplace that they used almost every night when there was a chill in the air. It was all on one floor and their bedroom walls held ceiling to floor bookcases. French doors from the master bedroom led them onto the veranda. The large bed was draped in mosquito netting and it added an intimate cocoon for their lovemaking. Meals were served in the dining room and Mutanda and Chisale, who had formerly worked in the Government House, were a perfect match to the newlyweds. They were excellent with organizing the daily living and with the marketing and Chisale was perfect for teaching Julia the in's and out's of the local village mores outside of their compound. In fact, it was Chisale who invited Julia to a meeting one day to see the women's cottage industries. It was through Chisale that Julia met Banti.

Their life began to take on a more normal existence and BB started to travel quite a bit in cataloguing his artwork. So that Julia was pleased when Chisale invited her to go on a tour of the area, stopping at the women's center in the local village. They walked a couple of miles down a sandy road to the closest compound.

Many think that African architecture is little more than mud huts. Mud, yes—but certainly not huts. Instead, these adobe buildings, many of them quite large to accommodate extended families, show sublime sculptural beauty, variety, and ingenuity. Many of the designs are still domed-shaped dwellings, surrounded by enclosed walls or fences. Not only was mud used as the main building material, but also local hardwoods. The roofs were often made of palm leaves or with hipped roofs of shingles. Perhaps the most striking and best known of local building was the key feature of courtyard-based buildings, and walls brightly painted with striking patterns.

As they entered the village, Chisale said to Julia, "I want you first to see the women's shrine and meet Mamy Wata. Perhaps

Banti will be here this morning and she is a very important woman for you to know. Especially for your writing."

They walked into a building that seemed to be a large room with a tiny office off to the side and it was all constructed from wattle and daub. The main room was in a circle and there were animal designs marking the walls. In the middle of the room was an altar and on it stood a wooden sculpture. It was known as Mamy Wata. This African diviner held a central place in the women's worship services, much as a Madonna and child might be found in any Catholic church. Julia was immediately drawn to the statue. Mamy Wata seemed a bit wild but majestic. She had snakes twined around her neck and her eyes were hypnotic. "What is she about," asked Julia.

"Banti knows all of the folklore around Mamy Wata, so I'll take you to meet her." Chisale suggested that they go to visit another village that was being built by foreign money. After that, she thought they could go to the large market and buy their fresh vegetables. On another day, Chisale said that they could go and visit some of the women running cottage industries in the area.

"This place that I am now taking you to was once a very poor village and illness was part of the everyday life. Now, it is being rebuilt as an experiment. I am told the idea is very simple. Every year for five years, the investors put money into the reconstruction and wait to see what happens."

"What do you mean, they wait to see what happens, and who are "they"?"

"You'll have to talk with Banti about the details, Julia, but I will give you a quick tour this morning. My understanding is that they are trying to take it away from the government and put it under privately owned controls. Specialists in all kinds of areas are gathering here, including HIV/AIDS research. Never before have I seen so much money being invested in a local community. So, they say that if this succeeds it will be an example for other developments in Africa. Come on, let's take this taxi so you won't get too tired or hot, and we'll have a tour. I think Banti is also there today."

They were taxied through dusty streets, past vendors selling their foodstuffs in front of what to Julia looked like shacks cobbled together from tin cans beaten flat and nailed onto wooden struts. Occasionally, Julia could make out the faded logo of the U.S. Agency for International Development on a rusted shell of an old vegetable oil can. Women in bright headscarves and second-hand clothes imported from America and Europe sold homemade snacks and Coca-Cola from wooden shacks dotting the sides of the red-brown dirt road. They were on the outskirts of the new village. The first building that they came to was a health clinic. The nurse there told Julia that each household received mosquito nets; and that the clinic also provided condoms and Depo-Provera contraception injections. They were about ready to administer anti-retroviral therapy. The patients walked to the clinic from other village's miles away. "We can always use some volunteer help if you have time. Julia said that she would definitely think it over but she was still a new resident and had first a lot to absorb. She was particularly interested in the school. So the nurse directed her to the green courtyard of a primary school. The red brick building had holes for doors and windows. But it lacked a roof. The teacher seemed embarrassed to tell Julia that it had blown off in a storm just a few days before. "Perhaps my husband and I can help to replace it, if you would like?" The teacher seemed very grateful because she knew that where Julia came from roofs don't blow off schoolrooms. "Well, that's not entirely true," and Julia went on to explain the damage that tornados do in her country. The teacher explained to Julia that they also had something similar to a head-start program where the children received a nutritious breakfast with necessary vitamins and protein.

When they arrived at the information center, Banti was there. "Hello, I am so pleased to meet you," said Banti. "We've been waiting for your arrival. I am looking forward to talking with you because I understand that you have an educational background?"

"Well, I have done a lot of writing on educational needs, and it is something that I am very interested in, and making sure that art is introduced into children's curricula." The so-called technology building was just a shack with a nice sign on the outside and a few books inside. "We are still wanting to be connected to a electricity grid, so that we can bring computers with Internet access. I personally would like to establish a cyberspace café and bring education in by long-distance learning. I want to build a center that will allow students access to unlimited information; their parents, also, will be able to obtain up-to-date reports on crop prices and fertilizers. Could I come and visit with you so that we could talk in more depth?" asked Banti.

"I would love it. Some day this week?" They agreed and Julia and Chisale started home, stopping first in the colorful market to get supplies. "This was quite a day, Chisale, and I want to thank you so much. Clearly, there are some questions I have about the business parts of the development program ideas, and for that I would have access to call in my friends who are experts in financial matters. Chisale told her that people feared and worried about any foreigners and their exploitations and she had heard about sporadic fighting that had been breaking out-- but the powers that be wanted to keep it quiet because they did not want any donors to pull out.

"I must remember to ask Banti about these questions. Do you think they'll be able to keep up the health clinic and school—what if the funding was withdrawn and the money ran out? My sense tells me, Chisale, that I have found a project to work with, but I don't know how BB will take it. Time will tell."

When she mentioned it to BB, Julia's sense was right, he did not take it well. "These are the donors that I must rely on to do business with, Julia." He feared there might be some repercussions or conflict of interests. It was the first chink in their points of view.

CHAPTER 9

THE BONDING THAT WAS OCCURRING between Banti and Julia was immediate and amazing. Within a month they seemed to have established a relationship that was deep. It was almost as if they were two very old souls who had actually known one another for several lifetimes. The fusion of their energetic minds seemed to be in total alignment, so it felt like a symbiosis of some sisterly connection.

"I feel as if you are a twin," Julia noted. "Do you understand what I mean?"

"Yes. I do. I think that we have shared another life together, no doubt more than one lifetime. Who knows, perhaps in that last life we were twins. This is the type of energy that is invisible to the eye. I suspect it comes from another form of reality not understood on the earthly plane. Those who study and believe in the knowledge that emanates from a Mamy Wata can often only understand this. It's as if we've been asked by the ancestors to complete a cycle. I am getting the sense that our purpose together is to bring a new level of consciousness to the world, and that it will manifest through the teaching company that we've been discussing that will be centered in our cyberspace café concept. It feels as if we are being asked to teach this new way of "knowing." Well, it actually isn't so new, but it has been lost due to the imbalances of the male and female energies. I do believe that this hunger for harmony and balance is lost with the greed for power over others; and the whole earth is reaching a critical mass in terms of healing the planet. We are in a time that puts the world, literally, on the edge of potential and terrible destruction not only for the planet, but also especially for Third World countries. It is the poor who always suffer the most."

"I've been having all kinds of dreams that suggest looking at a hologram as a model for understanding the cause and effect going on; and, you know, Julia, in my culture we call this unknown zone, karma. Civilizations come and go through the epoch of time. I have a strong feeling that our planet is reaching such a turning point.'

"Yes. I hear you. I have believed for some time now," Julia responded, "that it is in the power of the feminine—and by this I do not mean just in women—but it's a change that both men and women need to address—a major paradigm shift is underway so that it will no longer be the model of "top/down" starting with God and Man. In fact, I believe that the future depends on this shift. Perhaps that is why we've come together, Banti. First World and Third World women seemingly would appear to be at different ends of the spectrum. Still, if we can work out a collaborative model that can be replicated throughout the world—each of us bringing our strengths and cultural wisdoms that we have to offer---and to do it through the new technologies---well, I am beginning to realize this is a path where I want my own research to go. What is your vision of it, Banti?" "I truly agree that we must dramatically change directions."

"I think that when the financial markets begin to crumble in the first world countries, people might finally wake up---I just hope it is not too late. I see that the flow of consciousness needed will bring us into the depths of life's mysteries and a purpose and new transformation, and that is why I've been drawing on the need to reclaim the wisdom of the ancestors to synthesize the energies of the whole human being—male and female, alike—but learning how to express our higher purposes with the power that comes from within rather than that horrible power and control over everything."

"My vision," Banti went on, "is to start a school and use all of the new technology to reach many people, near and far. But I don't want it controlled by the World Bank or the International Monetary Fund with all of the constrictions and restrictions that they bring to the table. To me, they epitomize that power and control "over" everything and it reeks of the same old, same old days of the imperialists and colonialists who've, frankly, raped this entire Continent. It is no mistake that the current armies continue to use rape as their major power and control tactic to bring a village to its knees."

"I, also, have been doing a lot of dreaming" said Julia "and here is where I think the First World can help, but in new ways, and with the resources such as mirco-loans and the like for women running cottage industries. And, we must educate, educate, educate. Let's put together a business plan, shall we? I have two friends in mind that I would like you to meet. If I invite them, they will come. They are just the ones to help us with an economic development plan." Julia told Banti about Dominique Chantel and Arthur Nolan, two extremely wealthy and successful individuals with contacts worldwide, and her best friends.

Ironically, as the weeks went forward and Julia realized she had found her niche, she felt increasingly a deep level of focus in her own growth when connecting with the women in Owerri. Still, at the same time, she felt a pushing away by BB. She wondered if it might have some causal meaning in the fact that they were both only children and that Julia never had sisters. At first she thought it might be the natural adjustment to married life after the honeymoon is over and a couple starts to get re-involved with the normalcy of daily life. BB had been traveling a lot and was away for a couple of weeks at a time or out in the bush or tracing some kind of provenance on art objects. So no matter what, Julia would've had to fill her days with her own projects and interests. "Could BB be jealous?" she wondered. But she dismissed that thought as ridiculous since when he was at home and they were together, their sex life was still great. She did wonder and sometimes felt outside of his world as he never talked about it, and when she asked about his work he always seemed to redirect the conversation onto some other subject. Yet, there was a growing sense that she had of BB holding on to some kind of resentment about her integration with the women in Owerri. He definitely did not like it if she became involved in anything that was too political.

She was delighted when she heard that Charles and Dominique and Arthur would all be with them at the same time; but she was also worried about her father's health. Net had written that he'd had a TIA, a small stroke, and this had slowed him down. Julia asked if she should come home, but Net said not at this time and she would keep Julia posted as to Set's prognosis. " Both your father and I," wrote Net, "have agreed that your life is in Owerri before all else. Besides, we're not that badly off, we're just getting older!"

So for the next couple of months, Julia immersed herself in the upcoming plans both at the women's center and with her forthcoming initiation. She had been invited to become an initiate into the women's inner circle that was led by the wisdom of the shaman they worshipped and called Mamy Wata. All of this was being done under the tutelage of the women's group. She felt it a great privilege that the women at the center had invited her into their inner circle. She had Chisale and Banti to thank for breaking down any cultural or class barriers.

CHAPTER 10

HAVING BEEN IN THE MERCHANT Marines, BB, of course, had studied maritime history. He definitely knew, for example, that the French Corsairs considered themselves on a higher plane than mere pirates. In effect, the Corsairs used a form of legalized piracy and held government licenses, which gave them permission to plunder other merchant ships. Any booty taken was supposed to be shared with the authorities. But that was not always the case. So BB was not all that surprised when Charles Chantel e-mailed him with a proposition—for when they met in Morocco BB's first impression of Chantel was that he was a real adventurer/entrepreneur and maybe did not always play above the high-water mark. Yet, BB thought he was a good contact to have in Africa as he seemingly was connected with many tentacles moving out to the larger world on this continent, and beyond. As with the earlier Corsairs, BB could see Charles putting together an archeological expedition that he would invite him to join since BB had considerable experience at sea and with diving. Also, BB thought it might be a good opportunity to see what the players were doing with salvaged goods and found artifacts.

Charles invited himself to Owerri suggesting that he come at the time of his sister's visit because Dominique was planning to visit Julia, anyway, about some project with the women in the village. When they were all together, Charles said he would go over the details for the dive that would take place off West Africa near the Cape Verde Islands. All he said in his e-mail was that they would be diving for a sunken ship that had been torpedoed by a German U-boat during World War II. It was a Liberty ship and was then under transport to bring looted gold from Switzerland via Portugal to Dakar. No one had salvaged the cargo but Charles had been talking with a highly sophisticated French salvage company and their state-of-the-art technology that had been underwritten by some venture capitalists. He had come across some information about a cryptogram revealing the whereabouts of the ship that was alleged to hold a cargo not only of stolen gold, but diamonds and other artifacts. Charles had remembered when meeting with BB the day they drove over the High Atlas Mountain range that BB had been a specialist in the merchant marines in the deciphering of codes and other types of cryptic messages. That, in addition to his expertise in art history, was a tremendous asset for such a dive as this would be.

BB was intrigued. Thus far, he knew that at the end of 1939 and during 1940, as German armies marched into the Netherlands, Belgium, France and Poland, the amount of government-owned gold reserves were being transported out of harm's way to several ports, including Dakar in West Africa, for at that time Dakar was a French colony. There were also unknown quantities of private wealth and collections of art that had been designated to go into protection in a safe zone. But the cargo was being shipped during a period when German U-boats were already taking an enormous toll on allied shipping. Charles had learned, he told BB in his long e-mail, that it was one of those ships that was torpedoed and went down; but the mysterious thing was there was a cover-up to preserve the allies financial credibility. This Liberty ship had almost reached Dakar but just off Cape Verde she was struck. It took two more torpedo hits for her to sink.

According to Charles, one of the problems now was that if salvaged, there was a question as to who owned the rights to the cargo? Since it was a multi-national effort it was unclear. The United States Maritime Commission owned the ship, but she was in international waters and near a Portuguese colony heading to a French Colony. The legal question seemed to be: whose gold and whose jewelry and other artifacts should they go to? Also, the ship was carrying a mixed cargo that included 750 boxes containing gold bars that had been hidden in ammunition lockers; so it was inconclusive as to who might reap any profits from such salvage. Apparently, the ship was struck on her starboard side and all engines were stopped as the radio officer had time to transmit an SOS. The captain had given the order to abandon ship and all except three got safely into lifeboats. After the ship was hit two more times she appeared to break in two and sank with bow and stern ends up. The next day, a Dutch ship picked up remaining survivors. Charles had come across one of these survivors and from him he got the story of what was in the hull.

"But, as I reported," wrote Charles, "one of the problems we might encounter is that if we do have a successful dive we might also be entering an intense confrontation as to whom the booty should go. We will have to be very careful in this case. The dive that Charles wanted to do was being sponsored, he said, by an archeological association and partly by a private syndicate. These investors expect a return on their money. I want to warn you about this up front because it might involve more than a fun dive. So, think it over and we'll discuss it when I arrive in Owerri. In the meantime, if you know of any other investors—maybe Julia's father? — Write and let me know. I'm signing off for now, Charles.

BB thought it over for a day and then answered saying he was very much interested in such a dive. And, that he would ask his friend, Geno, who had made a lot of money in NASCAR racing. Set also had an Irish friend who liked to bet on the horses, but Set had not been well so BB did not want to contact him on this.

BB told Julia that Charles would be coming with Dominique and she was thrilled. So they started to make arrangements with Mutanda and Chisale. They re-arranged the cottage and got a pullout couch so all could fit. Dominique would have the guest cottage and Arthur Nolan could bunk with the other fellows, especially if Geno was also coming. They started making an itinerary and this would include a tour of the village and Mamy Wata's temple.

CHAPTER 11

Dear Dominique and Arthur,
I am writing you both in an attachment format. First of all, I am so excited that you are coming at the same time as Charles and that you are willing to help me with the women's projects. I'll put the fellows in a dorm situation and you, Dominique, in the guest room, and I'm sure it will all work out comfortably enough.
Secondly, I am pleased to hear that you are willing to invest in the cyberspace café. I have so much to tell you and I hope our time together will be very productive. Banti and I are putting together an action plan but we need your respective expertise to do a business plan. I think you are both going to love Banti. She is fast becoming the sister that I never had, and she has talent!
We simply must get her to Boston so she can finish her education and I would like you, Arthur, to take charge of this by setting up an internship for her at the company. That way, she will be on the payroll and act as my research assistant and she can help you with the fund development work. Setting up a cyberspace café as

a teaching company has long been her dream. She has so many wonderful ideas for her country and has already set up a steering committee of some very forceful women that I've met here. Talk about activists! These women are drawing me into their inner circle and I am learning so much!

In fact, I am starting to participate in an initiation to enter the inner wisdom of the women's circle. You will be fascinated to see their temple and learn about the divination of a diviner they call Mamy Wata. They own a beautiful sculpture of Mamy Wata and use this as a way of introducing younger women to this wisdom. This goddess has been a part of the African culture for a very long time; they are updating their ancient history by using Mamy Wata as a teaching tool on the subject of empowerment. You will both be intrigued by what I have stumbled upon here in Owerri—it is fascinating!

Arthur, I want you to find some wealthy investors in Boston and set up some micro-loans and grants and put it all in some type of trust for "green" projects here in Owerri. The women have found a new resource for cottage industries that will be sustainable. But, I need to warn you that BB is not too keen on this so don't talk about it in front of him. He's afraid that I am getting in over my head with local politics.

In fact, last week I joined the women in a protest. I am not sure I would call it a riot, as BB does, but that's his way of telling me to be more neutral. Sometimes, I think BB and I are drifting and I'm not sure what it yet means. He is frequently away, so what does he expect me to do with my time? His irritability about my new activities bothers me. I am also very worried about my Dad. Aunt Net reports that he is tired all the time and so maybe I will be coming home for a visit. Well, whatever and hopefully nothing will happen, at least not until after your visit. We can discuss all of this later.

But let me summarize what is going on with our cottage industry plans, as this is where I hope you both can play a part. It also is connected to the so-called "riot" because last week the women requested monies from the government's Ministry of Energy. They want the government to underwrite some grants for their latest project in setting up these photovoltaic technologies to use as a prototype for a cottage industry. The idea is to teach women in the village how to assemble the modules. The women will assemble the PV modules to also power small pumps to irrigate their herb and vegetable gardens. They also want to furnish this to use as power in our cyberspace café. Some of the women have already begun to make solar cookers, or stoves. They make these cookers out of cardboard boxes, aluminum foil and other inexpensive materials. Deforestation is a major issue because many of the trees are used directly for cooking and charcoal from the trees is sold to poor people for cooking fuel. But the efficient cook stoves run by photovoltaic technology and the idea is now spreading.

British Petroleum also wants to get into the act, but the women insist on having control of this developing industry. They believe that with creating solar panels for electricity in their own villages they will be able to expand into several other businesses. So the women shut down the government house last week when some of the local chiefs wanted a cut of the future profits. The women threatened them by using a shaming method of taking off their clothes! Talk about burning bras! The women were mostly middle and older ages. They blocked the entrances and they told the officials that if the government brought in soldiers they would have to shoot the women. So the military were told to stay at arm's length. It was really very funny, albeit tense to watch. The women also insist that their children get the jobs to build this new infrastructure and to keep the jobs of long-term maintenance.

The woman Banti has introduced to me is Jeanne. She is an engineer educated in the United States and she is the one who will be teaching the women about photo diodes and how to assemble them into modules. If they can build their own power station in the province, they will need more investment money. This is where we come in. I want you, Arthur, to setup some venture capital money to help. Also, get my father to invest, and all your other wealthy Bostonian friends. I know you can do it!

Well, this is a lot to absorb so I will sign-off for now. Dominique, I know you will be of invaluable help in setting up our cyberspace café and a business plan. In the meantime, don't mention to my father about the tension building up between BB and me. I can't wait to see you both, spend quality time together.

For now,
Love,
Julia

CHAPTER 12

THE RAINY SEASON WAS SETTLING upon Owerri so to make the time indoors useful BB and Julia began writing a book on the ethnology of West Africa. Julia served as BB's editor and in this way they gained back some compatibility. However, she was also spending more time at the women's center to begin her preparation for her initiation into what BB was calling "The Mamy Wata cult."

Julia tried to explain why it supported women's growth, but BB put it down to a lot of "voodoo." For the first time, Julia saw a real difference between them and it hurt as well as made her very angry when he told her she was in danger of losing her femininity.

"Whatever do you mean? I can't believe you said that."

"What I mean, Julia, is that you are a very sophisticated first world woman, and, for the life of me, I cannot see what women from a third world country have to teach you. Study their art, sure, by all means, but why are you falling hook, line and sinker into all of this rubbish?" Julia was flabbergasted.

"For a long time, BB, I have not explored my own spiritual path and I can see clearly and by comparison that I have led an extremely sheltered and spoiled life. Frankly, I've never had to think of anything but my own self. Certainly, I've not had to learn how to sustain my life. I feel that I have found a community that can teach me and I, in turn, can help offer resources. I can really make a difference in helping to find investors. I don't consider this a trivial thing, and I certainly do not understand what you mean when you say it is impacting on my femininity. I'm not walking around braless, for heaven's sake!"

BB laughed. "What's inside that bra is for me only, so don't you start parading around naked like your African friends were doing in that riot.

"BB, it was not a riot and you are making nasty and shallow remarks, and in my view, very racist. You sound like a typical American male and I find it very offensive. Besides, you are away so much and never talk about your life here, so what do you suppose I'm to do with my time?" Julia left the room in a huff.

She was increasingly worried about how they were getting into these spats but she thought maybe it was the weather and being so cooped up together. Julia realized that they had some things they would not be able to share together but she also knew that she was learning a great deal from her Owerri friends. In the morning when things cooled off she decided to talk with BB. So at breakfast she opened the subject again.

"Sometimes just getting started is the hardest part," said Julia, as she poured their coffee. "The only way I know how to begin is to be direct. I don't know what is wrong and I want to work on strengthening our relationship."

"Okay," said BB, "shoot. But before you begin, I need to tell you that I am feeling at a loss about how to become a better partner, especially with intimacy. I thought we were extremely close. Maybe my old definition of a man/woman relationship is dated and perhaps I didn't have a very good training with Helen and Will, and I'll admit there was a distance between them. But I'm really not sure that I can go "deep" as you call it. Nor, do I even know what you mean by "deep."

"Julia, has it ever occurred to you that you might be too intense? I like continuity and stability in our personal world. For heaven's sake, we are on a Continent that is filled with turmoil. Sometimes I feel that this need you have for getting involved gets too sticky. I don't like getting involved in public affairs. It doesn't mean that I love you less, either, when I feel the need for some distance. But, even if you are right about these emotional issues you won't win because I'm not into analyzing everything to death."

"I'm asking that you support my work with the village women and that you appreciate the initiation process that I am planning to do. But when you tell me it's just a lot of superstitious hogwash, I feel denigrated. Perhaps I have become overly reactive. One thing I'm realizing, though, is that I need to do some deep inner-work, and by that I mean a lot more introspection, especially about my parents. I do feel the need for solitude, too, when I attempt to go deeper into my past. You know, my mother died when I was only eight. Set was a dear and generous father, but he never shared much with me about his own life and I feel that you have some of those same tendencies. I know that you think being a Chilton is somehow the top rung of the social ladder, but I do not. I don't want my life to be designed by certain traits that you and my father think should be this way or that. Here, within the women's center I have the opportunity for the first time to discover my authentic self, rather than play a role of what is expected of me."

"You knew when you married me that I was an independent woman but now that I want to be more of an activist and be stronger in a new way, you accuse me of being less feminine. Doing this initiation is a big thing for me and it will require that I not only spend some time alone with my writing, but that I go on retreats at the Mamy Wata center. I need to go into the darkness in order to find the light."

"Julia, this is what I mean. What in hell are you talking about? This bullshit could be dangerous and it could change your personality. I don't want you to change. I want you just the way you are."

"Each of us must grow and change, BB. You make me want to cry because I thought you would want to climb the mountain with me, hand in hand. Now, I see that you do not."

"What the fuck do you mean, Julia? Climb what mountain? You know that I was never a religious person. In fact, I think religion has done more damage to this world than anything I can think of. The tribalism in this world and the conflicts between Muslims and Christians—the missionaries—all of it is hocus-pocus and it keeps these people from entering into modernity. Surely, you must see this?"

"You call me a first world woman and, yes, I sit on the board of a publishing company, and I edit books—but it's all been done through family connections and I've never had to start something on my own from scratch. Even now, I am counting on my family and friends and their financial securities to invest."

"When my mother was dying from advanced cancer--and I was protected from any painful information as to her prognosis because no facts were provided to me--I was completely shielded by Aunt Net and the word "cancer" was never used in my presence. When she died, I was dutifully led to the church to sit beside her closed casket. I never really grieved her death and I was whisked off to private school and lived a very lonely adolescence. My Dad distanced himself from everyone. Oh, sure…when he was around he would come down to a field hockey game, but mostly it was Aunt Net who covered for him. I don't want to make the same mistakes in our marriage; but quite candidly, BB, the longer I know you the more I see Set in some of your behaviors. You seem to be able to put everything into a category—a box. I mean, how can you study the culture here and not involve yourself with the people and their needs?"

"I'm not Carl Jung, Julia, and I didn't study psychology as you did. But I do know one thing that Jung said, and I agree with him…he said something about ultimately having to choose to live in one's own culture. You seem to want to become African. It's one thing to study the art but it's an entirely different kettle of fish to get involved with their daily living and cultural mores."

"BB, I'll think long and hard about what you are saying. But I'm still going to go ahead with this initiation and I'll need to stay at the women's center for the next two weeks, or, plan to do so whenever you go on your next field trip. That way, you don't have to become involved and this will be my thing just as your work is your thing. But it makes me sad to see us split in this way. Perhaps we can find that closeness again and maybe it works best when space allows a couple to do their own thing. Still, can you promise me to think about this conversation?"

"That's fine with me, Julia. I'm leaving for Nigeria next week. Okay? And I promise not to push your buttons. But think about this, Julia, perhaps the long and the short of it is that we both have to accept one another's differences."

Chapter 13

THE NEXT COUPLE OF WEEKS found Julia very busy preparing for her initiation and getting the action plan for their cyberspace café off and running. Banti had found the space and she wanted the center to be stylishly decorated with clean floors and a welcoming African décor. They would be expecting some computers being shipped by Arthur and Dominique—that would be a start. In terms of revenue intake one key feature would be a magnetic card reader attached to each computer. Customers would be able to purchase a card and pay in advance for as much Internet use as they wanted or could afford on any given day. In Owerri, they were estimating an hour's online time would cost about four US dollars. In this way, they hoped to build up a base of loyal customers who could sustain the café's overhead to support the students they ultimately wanted to serve. The ultimate goal was to begin long-distance learning on the World Wide Web. It would amount to a kind of debit card because many local villagers did not use a bank, but with the card that wouldn't matter. Anyone who could afford it would be able to walk into the café and buy Internet time that would underwrite the students for computer use. This is also where Arthur's investors would come in to help in building a reliable infrastructure. It seemed a bit risky, but it would be a start. To begin, the six computers coming would share a single telephone line. They hoped to open the cafe 24 hours a day, and with high-speed connections using solar panels they planned to produce electricity that would be even more cost-efficient. They hoped to make enough batteries to store and generate sustainable power. Eventually, they would link up to satellite high-speed reception but until such time as a fiber-optic undersea cable that the government was planning to bring in, they would have to work in stages. Their operation would be a prototype with plenty of room to expand. Profit margins would be slim at first; that is why Julia had suggested grants to get it off the ground. Julia also knew that Arthur could get monies from Boston area women to write some checks upfront. The proposal was a grand and huge undertaking, but Julia and Banti and Jeanne believed they could do it. Dominique was the one who had suggested that they set up a fund for micro-loans so that many people, especially women, could provide modest loans that helped their sisters in poorer countries become more self-sufficient. All of these ideas were off and running and when Arthur and Dominique arrived in Owerri, they would be able to establish the business plan with a foundation for the proposals to come together.

In the meantime, Julia was working with the women on preparing for her initiation. After fasting, Julia was told to keep a journal of each step in the process.

Week One

I am required to begin by weaving a piece of cloth that is said will be anointed to possess spiritual power. Cloth is used to celebrate major events. This cloth is important both for rebirthing and for burial rites. There is deep respect for—or fear of—the ancestors who are believed to hold the key to their descendants' fortunes. To show respect for the deceased, I am to wear a hand-woven cloth wrapped around my body. It is to be woven into vertical stripes across half the width, leaving the top white cotton. I can get help to do the pattern from an elderly woman in the village who is an expert weaver, but I must work on it, myself, at least four times a week.

Week Two

I must find some bones to shake during the ritual and to make a necklace out of the bones. The shaking of these bones is to hold the ritual as sacred and to help me remember where I come from in a long lineage of women who carry the lost wisdom. They are using some herb for helping my memory go back a long, long time ago--when I lived in former lives. When I drink their special broth with the herbs, the past is suppose to come up to my consciousness and I am told that I will feel as though I am watching my own movie, as if in a dream. When in a hypnotic like state, a voice will then ask: "Who are you?" "Why are you coming here?" "What is your gift to the world?" "What is your purpose here?" I need to respond as to what I believe that my special gift is. I am to open my channels to allow the wild woman shine through me, and I am not to hide her, or, my true being anymore. I have to learn how to teach in a new way, especially, how valuable women are in society. The world is not well and I have to learn that I am not just standing beside a statue because Mamy Wata represents not only the women of wisdom (such as a Sophia in the west is honored); but, what is different is that Mamy Wata is also a fecund being who is not afraid of her anger and who will confront negative forces and those that especially keep women down. Many developing countries, especially, have a long way to go in liberating women. The Taliban and other medieval belief systems are an example of this. When we take the tongue out of the mouth we cannot communicate. So, where do we find the gift of the tongue? I am told that I must go into my wounds to find hidden voices and to learn how to speak anew. When I feel as if I am getting stuck I must call on my sisters and ask Mamy Wata what the next step should be. In this way I will not feel lost or afraid and I can continue to examine how my soul and astral being is transforming.

I must do a lot of walking and learn how to astral journey from this world into and behind the hidden veil of the next world. I am told that I will learn how to use my body in new forms and ways. They say that I will even be able to walk right through the rocks as Mamy Wata could do and she will teach me how to avoid many hotspots, but I won't remember it when I awaken. It is a kind of surrendering into the rocks by discovering the energies that will allow me to become a carrier of Spirit. Sometimes these energies erupt like a volcano does; but other times the lava flows smoothly. Such an initiation can be dangerous because certain cells in my body will be dismantled so that I can go over to the other side. All of my senses will be opening. This will be a time of channeling. We will share food together in a bowl made out of bone. I will receive water from the elders who are the carriers of the water of life. The definition of an elder is "the thing that lasts." Another important aspect of the initiation is that I am to make friends with "Snake." When I have completed this initiation, I will be able to better mentor younger women and create a bridge between the spirit world and a more grounded existence on the earth. I will remember the gift that I am bringing forth, but I will not remember the details of each step in the initiation. It will be as if the whole experience was nothing more than a dream and I will intuitively trust to know what I must do in each situation.

Week Three

I have entered the shrine and I'm standing in front of Mamy Wata with my cloth wrapped around me. Ashes have been put on my face. This represents fire and the ancestors. I am entering five vibrations or five gateways or elements: The first one is the element of fire to connect me with the ancestors; the second element is water to bring focus out of chaos and to bring the energies into harmony; the third element is earth and with my bare feet in the earth I will be rooted with a sense of home and a ground of being; the fourth element is mineral. I am to hold onto rocks and tell a story about where I come from in this life and in other past lives, and to always remember where I am going. I am to use stones and bones and patterns in the earth and in the sky to help me restore all my lost history. Finally, the fifth element is about transformation and change in nature. This is the place where I can drop all masks and bring my true self with all of my breadth and depth into relationships. I will hold a bowl of water and stand in a circle with the other women who will be drumming and singing and dancing. I am to pour salt over Mamy Wata so as to seal and clean and feed the shrine. By knowing the Snake around Mamy Wata's neck I will come to understand how to use power. This will also support me in taking my many journeys into the other side. I will see my body from a place high above and a white light will surround me; but I will not be afraid even though it seems like death because the Snake is protecting me as I soul travel. I will be returning to the land from whence I came so that I can once again be reborn. Without a death and admitting that any day is a good day to die, I cannot accept that any day is a good day to live. The ancestors are telling me that they need me and that they cannot travel unless I am willing to join them in the journey. I am being told to forgive my parents and all of my ancestors and to release any resentments, grudges, or whatever is blocking me so that I can be ready when death comes. Then, I am to cut a vine and prune it so that I can replant my vine in nature. If my soul is bleeding I must grieve and forgive and let life energies flow. In this way I can cross back and forth into the land of the ancestors and to visualize my soul as being reborn into yet another life. In this life, I see a cup of tea with poison in it and part of me is aching. But as I cut the vine of this nightmare, I will feel renewable energy flowing back into my body, and I will be able to let the sap of life flow through me once again. As I come back into my body I will again feel very grounded and very peaceful and very connected both to the women in my circle and to all people in this present life. I will be ready to own my inner power and discover my gift and to share this knowledge with the world around me.

Chapter 14

THE MEN LEFT FOR THE dive, but Geno came back earlier than the others so Julia had a good opportunity to talk alone with him. There was something basic about Geno that she had trusted since first meeting him in Boston. She was very glad that he was BB's friend, and in his quarter. Geno was a person, she could tell, who saw things that BB often overlooked. Or, so she thought. Geno told Julia about the dive and how thrilling it was to see the mysterious little time capsules on the ocean bottom. And, at that moment of discovery when they first came upon the site and he had a turn to go down in one of those little subs—"It generated a sense of awe as I came closer and closer, and I could see an actual artifact lying on the ocean floor. It was magical. I can understand the adventure in it; but all the time I felt that something was wrong and that we were literally over our heads."

"In the second week, we were diving three miles out and off the coast of Cape Verde Islands. The salvage ship had some very sophisticated equipment that I knew nothing about. So I was mainly an observer. Charles seemed to take charge of just about everything. We had already brought up some artifacts that were found and they were wrapped inside tin boxes. Charles transferred these into plastic buckets and coded them before putting them into a small fishing vessel that we had towed. But, there was plenty more down there and the men reckoned it would be months before the work was completed. This was only phase one and a look to see what would be necessary for future dives. I was surprised that Charles brought up those few buckets and acted so quickly, to be honest. I never did have a chance to see what was in the boxes. The fishing vessel took them to an undisclosed place for security reasons, we were told.

"Later in the day we looked out on the horizon and sighted a Portuguese warship. Someone had apparently informed them about this dive, and they were investigating whether or not we had plundered what the captain said might belong to Portugal and to other governments, or so they alleged. The captain said that they were doing this intervention on behalf of a consortium. Anyhow, the whole situation was getting dicey and a group of officers boarded our ship and examined all of our passports. They said that they were commandeering the ship and planning to take it into port at Cape Verde Island. Charles argued vehemently with the ship's officers."

"But Charles had already stripped our vessel of whatever artifacts had been pulled up and put in those tin boxes and he told us that to protect our own security it was best that we didn't know too much. At this point, I began to feel really antsy about the whole deal. Especially when the salvage boat was ordered into port. Then, after an hour where we were told to dock, Charles went ashore an called some lawyer because he had been charged with "severe disobedience to a foreign government ship." The lawyer posted bail and Charles is supposedly now free. I got off and headed back here. BB stayed behind to sort things out with Charles and the others. The fact is, Julia, I don't know what the hell was going on or where Charles stashed those plastic buckets."

"Does BB?" Julia asked.

"I don't know. But they're both due back here in a few days. I need to get back home to attend to some business, so I left early. At first I found the dive exhilarating but as we got dragged into all this legal crap I wanted to get out. I'm sure some of the other investors are going to feel the same way."

"So, you don't know what they found?"

"There certainly were some gold bars and we pulled up a few; but there's a helluva' lot more down there. I think that booty is what will be held up in the maritime courts for some time to come. We also pulled up artifacts that included some jewelry but, again, I did not have a chance to view any of it. Somebody said they thought jewelry belonged to survivors of the Holocaust because during the war years the Swiss wanted to get all the assets they could out, and the fastest way was on a convoy such as this. It is known that the Swiss did try to smuggle some of this stuff out through Portugal for security reasons, but who benefits today from such a cache is beyond me. Apparently the Portuguese ship was acting on behalf of other countries because they were the closest to Cape Verde Islands, and they knew the language there, and so on. It was suggested that a class action suit would be brought against the salvage company, and that the plaintiffs might include the United States government. Frankly, it is beyond me how BB ever got himself caught up in all of this."

"What you've told me is quite astounding, Geno. So what is your overall impression, now, of Charles?"

"I don't trust the son-of-a-bitch for one second. I told BB this, but he shrugged me off. I'm telling you, Julia, this is a complicated situation. Some of the specialists aboard who study shipwrecks and their cargo told me that treasure hunters have been accused of destroying wrecked sites in search of valuables and criticized for selling the salvage through auction houses and even on the Web. It's a new kind of smuggling and it moves very quickly. BB seems very interested in this side of the story and he plans to investigate it more thoroughly. As for Charle's intentions, I don't really know if he is that altruistic but I do know that he has many investors to answer to at this juncture. So I don't know if he is only out for the buck. My instincts tell me to watch this guy closely. He's almost too smooth, but no treasure hunter is going to spend the time and the money if he has to pay off investors. I just don't know, Julia. As I said, I came along for the ride and to try and find some investors for my own schemes, but for now I will just keep quiet and watch how this all unfolds. I only hope that BB isn't getting in over his head."

"Thanks for sharing this with me, Geno. I really appreciate your being so candid."

"The thing of it is, Julia," Geno went on, "some of the group aboard have a lot of money, and the salvage company, itself, has been using archeologists to excavate wrecks by forming limited partnerships with them—the salvage company even offers governments the technology necessary for salvaging their actual histories from the depths by offering to shoulder the financial burden of excavations in return for a cut of the proceeds. The truth is these professional salvage companies can do things that no government in the world can do. That's why I can't figure out why Portugal has become so embedded. It almost feels as if someone alerted the Portuguese navy and set it up and blew the whistle on this dive. Why? Besides, I was told that between 1939 and 1945 Portugal received at least 123 tons of looted gold directly or indirectly from the booty in these convoys, and what's on this particular ship is now in contention. I thought that it belonged to the salvage company, well; it made me wonder what the hell I was doing there instead of our own navy. Secrecy pervaded nearly every aspect of this dive and it bugs me that I don't know where the buckets we did pull up are going to be stored. I'll leave that for BB to figure out. Perhaps he'll stick around to find out the whole thing going on with this, and maybe we'll get our cut, but maybe not. Frankly, I now doubt it. It could perhaps be a complete tax write-off for all that I know. Hell, win some lose some. As I've said, I just mainly came along for the ride and because BB asked me to tag along. So, I did. That's about all that I can tell you at this point. Mutanda is going to drive Arthur, Dominique, Banti and me to the airstrip so we can catch our flights so I need to finish my packing. Julia, if you need me for anything or BB gets in trouble, here's my business card with my e-mail address on it. Call me anytime day or night. Watch out for BB, okay?"

"Okay. Thank you for being such a loyal friend. I'll stay in touch." They gave one another a hug and Geno left to pack up.

Saying goodbye wasn't easy for Julia. She told her friends that she was due to make a trip to the States very soon because she needed to see her father and she thanked them for all they were doing. She felt sad but happy to see Banti going off with Arthur and Dominique to do the work that was needed. Julia waved as the plane took off and stayed to watch until it disappeared behind the clouds.

When Julia got home the house was very quiet and she felt very lonely. She was also exhausted and decided to take a nap. Her dreams started up again. For the first time, she awoke feeling an intense fear of an unknown presence.

CHAPTER 15

CHARLES AND BB RETURNED FROM the dive the following afternoon. Both of them were tired out and Charles said he needed a couple of days to rest before he left. BB was sick. He had been hit hard by what appeared to be some type of virus. On the second morning, Charles said he was going out to the market and then he would pack up and be on his way back to North Africa. It was very quiet for several days and Julia did not say anything as BB was sleeping most of the time being under the weather and quite wiped out. He was still running a low grade fever and the doctor took blood tests. He thought it might be mononucleosis. Or, malaria. Julia stayed by his side to nurse him.

Charles said that he had to get on the next plane and he didn't have time to stay and talk. Besides, he didn't want to get sick. He told Julia not to worry about him and that he was making his own arrangements to get to the airfield. "I'll try to get back in about a month; but right now, I have a lot to do." So, before she knew it Mutanda gave Charles a ride to the airport. In truth, she didn't know what to think of Charles. But he seemed extremely nervous. At the moment she didn't care and was only worried about BB and her father because Net had sent a wire telling her that Set had been hospitalized at Massachusetts General with a heart attack but was resting comfortably in the CCU. The prognosis sounded fairly good, and if she could come home---now might be the time.

That afternoon Chisale ran into the house and cried out that Mamy Wata was gone missing. "I went in to clean the temple and Mamy Wata was not there. She's disappeared. Nobody else in the village has seen her nor has anyone been seen near the shrine. As you know, we never lock the door."

Julia was as shocked as was everyone in the village. But she tried to stay calm and needed to prioritize what to do. Julia's father was in a Boston hospital and when BB awoke she talked it over with him. BB said she needed to get to Boston right away and that Mutanda and Chisale would take care of him. Mono, after all, he said, simply means a lot of rest. As she automatically went through the paces to get ready to leave, all that Julia could think about was her last dream. She had a foreboding about the events unfolding.

CHAPTER 16

JULIA FLEW INTO BOSTON AND went straight to the hospital. Her father was resting comfortably after what he called a mild heart attack, and Aunt Net was sitting knitting beside him. The doctor came in and told Julia that he was going to make it. The prognosis looked fairly good. He would be sleeping on and off for the next week as he was highly medicated and it was just a matter, now, of waiting as he gathered up strength.

The big surprise that night, however, was the telephone call from Arthur. He had just received a call from Dominique who reported that in her issue of this month's ART NEWS that had just come in the mail there was a review of the next exhibit to be mounted at the L.A. County Art Museum. Mamy Wata from Owerri was to be the featured sculpture. How could this be? Wasn't this the sculpture they had seen in Owerri and the one Julia and Banti embraced? Perhaps it is another one? Maybe there were several sculptures floating around. Odd, though.

Julia immediately asked Arthur and Banti to join her in the Louisburg Square house and then put a call into Dominique in New Mexico. That night the four of them held a conference call and hatched the plan to go to Los Angeles and steal Mamy Wata as soon as the exhibit opened. After the deed was done, Julia would converge with the others at Dominique's hacienda in New Mexico. Julia told Net that she would be gone about a week, and upon her return Set should then be back home.

***

All was in freefall as everyone gathered at the hacienda, and as scheduled they all arrived at approximately the same time. Julia had been in deep thought all morning and had made her decision as to what she would do. She announced that she would head to Boston to talk with her father before going back to Owerri. She planned to take Mamy Wata with her. The others could wait for Ketu to come and begin the investigation.

She said nothing to any of them about the dive, or what she was beginning to suspect. She only knew that as soon as possible she needed to talk with Set. Julia told them to keep the diamond and the code safe until Banti's brother arrived, and then to tell him everything that they knew thus far. Before Ketu Tutola returned to Owerri, she suggested that he call and come to Boston to talk with her father, and to definitely come and see Julia as soon as he was back in Owerri.

When Julia arrived back in Boston, Set was home with a nurse taking charge of his aftercare. He was weak but alive, and very pleased that Julia had come. Aunt Net was also relieved. The three of them had a quiet dinner together and then Julia told Set that she would talk with him in the morning after breakfast. She told him that she needed his advice.

The following morning after Set was made comfortable, Julia closed his door and told him that she needed him more than ever. She shared with him everything that had happened. Set listened very attentively and when she was finished, he closed his eyes.

"Let me digest all of this for a few moments, Julia. First of all, I am glad you are here and that you have been willing to share all this information with me." With closed eyes Set became very quiet. Silence remained in the room for what seemed like a long time. Julia waited patiently.

"The first thing you should know," as Set finally looked at her and spoke, "is that the Chantel family is a very complex one. It's most important for you to also know that Dominique, like you, was deliberately kept in the dark all of the years of your growing up. Her father and I felt this was the way we could best protect you both. As for Charles, he was always a loose cannon and even as a teenager was off on one harebrained scheme after another. I know his father was very worried about him, for he was a very willful kid.

"Now, in terms of the lost gold. Yes. It is true that I was in the OSS and later joined the CIA and became head of the art squad until I reached an age where I no longer needed or wanted the responsibility. However, I was asked to continue to recruit candidates, and I have done so. Julia, I am going to divulge a secret that you must never share with anyone. Can I trust you?"

"Yes, Dad."

"You do not have to mistrust your husband. The reason he cannot share with you what he is doing is that he is under top security clearance and is working for the United States Government. I am telling you this so that you do not let it interfere with your marriage. But that is all that I can tell you. Do you understand what I am saying to you, my daughter?"

"I think so."

"The third thing you need to know is that the World War II Liberty Ship did, indeed, go down and that we were chasing the Portuguese as to what they knew from the very beginning. We knew that the Swiss were transferring loot and our government was involved in a secret operation to get it to a safe place in Africa. There is a lot of smuggling still going on, and that is one of the reasons BB is assigned to Owerri. It sounds to me, from what you've told me, that he is very close to figuring out what we've wanted to know for quite a while. My child, go back to your husband and stop being suspicious of him. He is doing a very difficult job and you must not doubt his loyalty either to his country or to this family. In fact, you need to also know that I am a proud American so no matter what you may have heard about me in the past, I have always remained a patriot. I am getting to the end of my life now, Julia. And it's been a good and a very adventurous one. But I have to tell you that the most wonderful thing that ever happened to me was meeting your beautiful mother, and bringing you into the world. I was devastated when the cancer came and I admit that I was no doubt a very poor father, but I have always loved you. I am also very proud of you, Julia. But now I am very tired and need to rest. My advice to you is to go back to Owerri with your sculpture and let things unravel, as they most certainly will. I give you my blessings and my love, sweetheart."

With that, Set said he was exhausted and needed to sleep. Julia went to her room and wept. She felt that it might be the last time that she would see her father. But she also felt very relieved at what she knew was a hard thing for him to divulge. She was eager to get back to Owerri, and to BB.

She tried to digest all that her father had told her. Apparently, Switzerland was the primary country that had received stolen gold from the Third Reich. Nazi Germany used stolen gold in order to pay for needed raw materials, such as tungsten, while Portugal was eager to increase its gold reserves. The Swiss National Bank served as one of the main launderers of this looted gold from the Third Reich. After the war, the Allies demanded the return of 44 tons of this gold, most of this being from the Belgian national reserves. However, Portugal consistently refused to hand over more than four tons, claiming that there was no clear evidence that the gold had been acquired illegally. "This is a real labyrinth, her father had told Julia, and it goes back a very long time. This particular convoy, I don't know, as I understood it, was not to be held by the Portuguese so I am not sure why they are claiming a stake. However, all roads now lead to Charles, as it was his father who was put in charge of the operation. I know that Jim Vogel also worked on this during the war. Maybe Charles knows something and is hiding it from the rest of us. I need to do some investigating of my own. In the meantime, Julia, go home to your husband. I will be in touch." Set remembered his exact words to his daughter and it broke his heart.

Chapter 17

Julia was so relieved to learn about BB and felt terribly of her suspicions. The poor man was under a lot of stress and she was unable to help him. So Julia returned to Owerri with Mamy Wata and placed the sculpture under secure guard in the women's temple. BB was back on his feet but was at a regional meeting with Mutanda and wasn't due back for a day or so. That evening she was sitting on the veranda watching as Chisale walked down the path for her evening out to stay with her sister. Suddenly, Charles appeared from the bushes and Julia was surprised. Chisale had left the teapot simmering and when they were alone Charles offered to bring in the tea. Returning with a pot he slowly poured a cup for Julia.

"You know, Julia, you are a very smart woman and I could tell when we got home from the dive that you were putting the pieces together. I think you know why I'm here. I want the diamond and the cryptogram."

"But I don't have them, Charles. I had no idea you would go to such extremes."

"Nor did I expect you to do the same in recovering your precious Mamy Wata. I need to know where you have hidden things as I have a lot of investors breathing down my neck and I need to pay them off as soon as possible."

"What I don't understand, Charles is why? You certainly have enough money and it was very foolish of you to steal Mamy Wata."

"Perhaps. I had no idea you and my sister would stick your noses into this. Excuse me, Julia, but we need more hot water. I'll be right back."

"The one thing I've not figured out, Charles, who is your middleman?"

Pouring the tea into her cup, Charles said, "I suppose it doesn't really matter if I tell you everything. The fact is that my consortium has been involved in smuggling art out of several countries, including Africa, for some time now. I could not have been successful without Jim Vogel. He is my middleman, and he and our fathers have been doing business together as far back as World War II when they were all involved with the OSS. Jim approached me some years back and made it sound so simple. Except, then your father had to send BB over here and that's when it all got mucked up. I figured BB had real suspicions when we were on the dive. When we returned, the most logical place that I thought of to hide the diamond and the code, and, by the way, the code is very important because it tells us a lot about the provenance. I thought, how convenient, Jim could get the sculpture of Mamy Wata into the L.A. County Art Museum very quickly, and we could let things cool off before we sold it outright. We had to let things calm down because of the legal discovery issues associated with the dive. I did not think that it all would become so complicated. At least that was the whole idea before you and my sister interfered with the damn sculpture."

"Charles, you must turn yourself in. Why were you so greedy?"

Suddenly, feeling light-headed, Julia put down her teacup. "What have you put in this tea, Charles?"

"I'm very sorry, Julia. I promise that it won't be painful. You will simply fall asleep and no one but us will ever know. Ironically, the tea is from a sticky African sap that is known as Bride's Flower."

"I would not have thought you would turn to murder. This is a strange déjà vu because I've been having dreams about BB and tea and some kind of evil hanging over us. What makes you think I've not already told BB and my father? The diamond and cryptogram is not in my possession nor is it inside of Mamy Wata. This has all been for nothing."

"I don't believe you, Julia. By the time you are asleep I shall be long gone. No one will ever know I was ever here."

Julia started to feel increasingly dizzy. "Come, Julia, my dear, let me help you into your bed. You will soon be asleep and in your sleep you will tell me where the diamond is."

"You foolish man, it won't work. Killing me is senseless and my father will never let you get away with it. Not only that, Charles I know a whole lot more now and I will come back. It might not be in this lifetime, but we will meet again in another lifetime."

"Julia, you see, you are beginning to hallucinate. Come, soon you will be sound asleep and I will be far away—long gone from Owerri."

CHAPTER 18

WHEN CHISALE ARRIVED HOME THE next day she found Julia unconscious in her bed. By the time she called the emergency people it was clear that Julia was dead. The medical examiner reminded them that a body in Africa decomposed very quickly due to the temperature, and if there were any traces of an unknown substance to be found it might be too late. Chisale finally tracked down BB and Mutanda. Mutanda was totally speechless and said he would bring BB home immediately. As best he could, Mutanda would tell BB on the ride home. They were numb and drove straight through to arrive late that night. BB was in shock. They could see him crumble right before their eyes. Chisale told him that they had to get the body cremated and she made the arrangements as BB followed in a post-traumatic and almost comatose state. BB was completely undone in a deep grieving. Two weeks passed. Mutanda arranged the trip to Boston as BB went through the motions in a zombie state. By the time he flew to Boston, BB was in a deep depression. He had brought Julia's ashes home to Louisburg Square, but BB was in a ghost-like trance and could barely talk to anyone. Set and Aunt Net were also traumatized. Geno, Arthur, Banti and Dominique arrived. A memorial service was held in the Brimmer Street church and Arthur and Banti gave the eulogies. They buried Julia next to her mother in Mount Auburn Cemetery in Cambridge, Massachusetts. Family and friends were completely devastated. Net had put black crepe over the mirrors and a funeral wreath was hung on the front door. The house went into deep mourning. Each in their own way was having a terrible time in their bereavement. BB was riddled with guilt and remorse for not listening to Julia and not sharing more with her. When Ketu arrived from New Mexico the men huddled in Set's study for long periods of time. No one seemed to know what to do. Except, Set. He was haunted by the fact that he had sent Julia back into the hands of her murderer. Of course, he thought BB would be home. Set struggled to regain his last bit of strength and then, after talking with Ketu, he went into action. Ketu told Set that he had the diamond and the cryptogram and they were doing tests on it now. Ketu also went to the L. A. County Art Museum and traced a bill of lading back to Columbia University in New York City. Ketu had already contacted Interpol to check what they might have. It seemed that they had been undercover with Charles Chantel as a person of interest for sometime, but there was as yet no concrete evidence to bring him in. They even had Set under observation but Jim Vogel had as yet to come onto the radar screen. He had suggested that Set and BB try to de-code the cryptogram and Ketu would return to Owerri with the diamond. Ketu was not sure to whom the diamond now belonged; but said that he would be turning it over to the Maritime salvage investigators.

Set retreated more deeply into his study. He spent hours trying to figure out each step. But BB was not in any condition to concentrate. Set played the bereaved father and did not want Jim Vogel to know what was going down although it made him sick to receive a sympathy card. Thankfully, he was busy and could not come to Boston for the service. Set had another and faster option to focus upon. He called up Mike Murphy in Dublin and asked him to come to Boston as fast as possible. Set mostly sat in silence and waited and BB thought he was sleeping, but he was not. He was thinking. In a couple of days, Set announced that Mike would be arriving and that Mike could muster in Set's people. But he did not want BB to be here. He arranged for Geno to take BB away for a few days. Set had persuaded BB that a long weekend on Vinalhaven would be good for him—Maine was one of Julia's favorite places and it could be a healing place, right now, for BB to be up there. He asked Net to accompany them.

When Mike Murphy arrived, he contacted Sal Vitori. Geno was leaving that day to drive to Rockland and then they could get the ferry over to the island. When Geno arrived at Louisburg Square he found that they were huddled in Set's office; Aunt Net—in her own deep grief—stayed out of the way and was packing to go up to the island. She had coffee and sandwiches and cookies brought in to Set's study and then she disappeared upstairs. It was clear to Geno that Set would not be with them too much longer; he looked like a skeleton already. BB looked like hell, too. He sat brooding in one corner of the room. But Set still had a determined look in his eyes. He was relieved when they all departed for Maine. Then, he turned to his loyal followers.

"There are two jobs that I want you to do for me before I die. I am ready to go to my beloved wife and daughter, but not before this is done. I have been thinking for some time now, and I have a plan. I need the old team to make it happen. I want Geno protecting BB, as always. I've been talking with BB about what he needs to do to get a new life started. He vaguely talks about how he and Geno have often discussed buying a schooner and sailing the seven seas. Well, I have an even better idea. When I'm gone there will be plenty of money to take care of Net. She gets this house and the rest is already assigned to philanthropy. But there will be Julia's estate and it is sizeable and it will go to BB. I want Geno to take BB to the Seychelles and buy a schooner. The two of them can start up a diving business. I've been doing a lot of thinking about it and it all works out in my mind.

"Sal, I want you to come up with some diving scheme with big money and then invite Charles Chantel to join you on the boat. He does not yet know we're on to him so say something about finding a lost ship filled with artifacts. I don't give a damn what you use for an excuse, but get him there. So far, the medical examiner has deemed Julia's death due to a coronary heart attack. Chantel thinks he has gotten away with murder. BB is not to go anywhere near Chantel, do you understand? Nor is Geno. You fellows are to track Chantel every single minute. Geno is to stick like glue to BB. I don't care what crazy schemes you have to come up with but do it, and make Chantel think we are simply grieving and BB is trying to rebuild, but he has gone into isolation with his loss. Tell him that everyone is shocked about Julia having a heart attack. That is all. Make up excuses on how to get him to the Seychelles. The rest is up to you and your crew, Sal."

"I've been reading in reports that I get from the Bureau that there's been a lot of piracy in the Indian Ocean. I don't mean pirates of old, either. I'm talking about the pirates of today who are seizing yachts and tankers off the coast of Somalia. One report I read had these pirates storming a luxury yacht as it was going out of the Seychelles towards the Mediterranean. The ship was in the Gulf of Aden. Pirates seized more than two-dozen ships last year, and the French government has also been investigating. Sal, there are plenty of sharks in those waters. So you and the boys know what to do when you get Chantel aboard. You get my meaning?" Sal nodded.

"As for Vogel, Mike--that's up to you and your Irish boys. I don't want to know any of the details and maybe I'll be dead by then, anyway, but do the job. The son-of-a-bitch is now more than a traitor to me. I want him eliminated."

"BB, needs a lot of time and he won't have to worry about money. I think the sea will be the most healing thing imaginable for him now, and I know that Geno will stay with him as long as he is needed. I also want you to talk with Arthur and Banti and Dominique. Especially Dominique. Never let her know about her brother. Mike, I want to give them a big endowment for the Owerri Women's Center so that they can get the cottage industries and the cyberspace program fully off the ground and running so that no one can ever interfere with it. I want it named the Julia Chilton Brewer Institute, under some goddamn non-profit thing--as that way it will all be protected and no goddamn government can interfere with its work. I want Banti put in charge of the whole program. Arthur and Dominique will serve as board members. This is what Julia would have wanted. So, Mike, I'm putting you in full charge. Now, does everyone have his orders? I'm tired and I need to go and rest but I'm still the godfather of this cartel and my orders are to be followed. Mike, you call in the legal minds and figure it all out. I'm going to make you my durable power of attorney so you can sign off on all the legal work. This will no doubt be my last order. Does everyone understand?"

CHAPTER 19

BB AND GENO BOUGHT A 46' gaff-rigged schooner. It was a classic yacht that they found in Southern Spain. The hull was wooden. It was a fore and aft Staysail schooner. She had a raked stern with bowsprit and a raked curved transom. The vessel had recently gone through an extensive refit, including refurbished masts with standard rigging, and a whole new diesel engine with the latest state-of-the-art electronic system aboard. The boat had two double berths and three single berths. There was a head, shower and Press water, a purified water system. The galley had a diesel stove, sink, freezer, and Nova cool refrigerator. The booms and masts were solid fir.

They sailed her to the Seychelles in the middle of the Western Indian Ocean between 4 ° and 5° and 55° and 56° E, 575 miles from Madagascar 980 miles from Mauritius, 990 miles from Mombasa and 1,748 miles from Bombay. The area included mountainous granite and three coral islands. The climate was hot and moist in a tropical atmosphere. The mean temperature varied from 75° to 86° F at sea level. As the relative humidity was high, averaging seventy-five to eighty percent all the year round, the stream off the S-E monsoons brought largely a cooling effect. Fortunately, the Seychelles were outside the cyclone belt for the Southern India Ocean, thus, spared the storms from which many of the Southern islands periodically suffered.

The overall lay of the land was lush tropical vegetation overlooking white beaches and clean lagoons. All along the coast of the main islands were small villages and many of them were fishermen's shacks made up of thatched cottages, often built on rocks piled up on each other, and facing the sea. Many of the villages retained their French names.

The town of Victoria, the old Etablissement du Roi of the French, was situated on the east coast of Maké, with a small but good port, protected by a ring of islands and islets. Due to colonization there was a Portuguese, French and British flavor to the Seychelles.

Most of the flora consisted of botanical treasures such as Seychelle palms; the great broad-leaf forest hardwoods; screw pines; orchids; the curious pitcher plant; and the jellyfish plant which is the rarest and the most distinct of the whole of the Seychelles plants. Early explorers had left vivid accounts of the beauty of the forests from sea level to the top of the highest mountains and tourists loved the large number of colorful birds and large crocodiles and tortoises that abounded.

The people were loving and harmonious and had achieved an outstanding society originating from Europe, Africa, Madagascar, China and India. The French language was molded in an African syntax, or Creole with a French patois. A majority of the people were Roman Catholic; still, the old ways continued and the Seychellois' fear of the supernatural continued, in spite of over a quarter of a century of Christianity, and their rituals with the indigenous folks permeated throughout the islands. There were still witch doctors and diviners who acted as healers and herbalists. One African custom that had survived was a popular communal dance known as "moutra." It was a nocturnal gathering around a fire, and the dance was accompanied by the throbbing beat of the African drum. The dance was a lament, and the participants gave the narration of a story afterwards. In time, BB attended these gatherings and found them very healing. It was in this way that he was able to tell Julia's story of Mamy Wata and it was accepted and welcomed by the people.

From studying the folklore, BB learned about various shipwrecks and sea adventures with pirates. He couldn't recall when he actually started to write his stories, and he was amazed when a British publisher picked them up. Over time, he became a very well known author using the name of William Brewer. In this way, he was able to also write Julia's story. But he never returned to Owerri. And no one ever mentioned Charles Chantel.

Geno flew back and forth about three times a year. They had started a diving school business and hired a manager to run it. They offered diving courses from beginners to advanced classes. BB also learned underwater photography and he enjoyed that work more than running the actual diving business. But mostly he lived aboard his schooner, and wrote stories. His schooner was named the "Julia."

One day BB went to the post office to check for any mail in his box. There was a bulky package that had Chisale's return address from Owerri. He went back to the boat and after brewing a pot of coffee, settled down in the cockpit and opened the package.

Julia's Journal

"Let me tell you, dear muse, about the day I learned there was a Mbari Temple in Owerri. I was sitting on my veranda reading the local paper and there was an article about re-dedicating the temple to the local deity known as Mamy Wata. Although I knew little about her, except what I had heard from the women, I wanted to know more. Mamy Wata was known as "the black goddess" and she held a special role as a diviner. I became fascinated with her image, as Banti had told me about her. She would introduce me to the Mamy Wata rites. Like Medusa, Mamy Wata had a snake wrapped around her neck.

"At first glance, Mamy Wata came across to me as a devouring mother with wild stringy raffia hair and bulging eyes. She looked rather crazed. A closer look, however, revealed something deeper; and, as I learned more from the women at the center, I came to see that she was so much more than the mother figure, and that, actually, she was not the devouring mother, but the raging woman as well as the transformer. She is as black as ebony and creates a vortex of energy, which is sometimes chaotic and often peaceful, and depicts all of creation. To her devotees, she is like a black sapphire---a very fine jewel radiating rays through her blackness as the women dance and sing and laugh with abandonment when they are in her presence. There is an intoxicating sexuality about her and the mystery she evokes is far different than the Madonna and child in our western iconography. This goddess is a full woman in both her fecundity and her spirituality exuding enormous power."

"I have been doing a lot of research on this phenomenon and perhaps what frightens people about her is that she creates tensions between the masculine and the feminine. I see this happening already in my marriage. I know that BB does not understand what is happening or why I am taking this tack. I recognize that my words will actually lend themselves to each individual's interpretation. Most educated people will dismiss all of this as unknowable, and simply the vivid imagination of a dreamer. These experiences challenge our rational view of the world. Perhaps others might accept the possibility of spirit ancestors, and I know that many people will understand reincarnation. But others might argue that all religions are superstitious, and that any such confused beliefs in spirit gods are not real. I see so many doubts, particularly in the fear that represses and frightens men and their suppression of women. It is, I believe, a fear that men have about women's inner power. This necessitates their need to control power over women. In other words, women are bluffed by this controlling power, and they fear the physical abuse that comes with it, so I see how we each—man and woman--disassociate from our own deeper selves. This happened to me because after all, I was taught to be a New England bred lady."

"What I have learned from Mamy Wata is that we each must go through a death of the ego in order to be transformed into the light of the control that comes from within. This means a letting go of false values, of the clinging that we all do in order to feel safe from death—death of any kind. Mamy Wata taught me that in the burial ground of the heart, we women see not only the death of the patriarchy that is rooted in fear, but the death in our own selves and the false assumptions under which women have also lived. Mamy Wata has taught me that it is the power from within that we need to aspire to, rather than power over---all things, and when I learn this lesson—and it is a karmic one-- I will be on an evolutionary spiral with no knowing of where it will end?

In order to stay grounded in this work, I have to return to my own western poets and this is a truth that BB knew. We do have to honor our own cultural background. I have been reading the poetry of T.S. Eliot who said in his _Four Quartets:_ ----'there is only the dance.' Once we learn this, we will all be free of the fear of the Great Mother and of death, free of our own vulnerabilities. What could we accomplish if we were all free of fear and the need to try and possess and control all of nature? I believe we will then only honor one another and learn how to hold the Earth sacred, too.

"Someday, perhaps all of this might get published and I will leave it to a future time; but for now I simply want to tell my muse, what I have been learning. I see that Mamy Wata represents the constant cycle of things, perpetually destroying, and, at the same time, she is creating---destroying in order to create, creating in order to destroy, death in the service of life, reality and life in the service of death. This is the continuum. Mamy Wata is time, she is immanence, ceaseless becoming----she symbolizes nature as a process. She is indifferent to the demands of the ego. The opposites of life and death, love and hate, humility and pride, poverty and riches, mercy and revenge, justice and tyranny---they mean nothing to her, because with Mamy Wata there is no polarity. All experience is one---life as well as death.

"In the villages where Mamy Wata is celebrated, the women spend weeks shaping a clay statue of their beloved goddess. She, who is the feminine wisdom deeply, held within the body, which makes no sense in the light of raw rationality, can be found by balancing our deepest selves. I can see how this might be difficult for many men who've been socialized to the logical and the deductive.

"When her feast day arrives, the women sing and dance from deep primordial roots, and they carry Mamy Wata through the streets, just as if it was a southern Italian town in Sicily carrying the blessed virgin. But the difference is that this goddess is not pure, not virginal, as was Mary, Mother of Christ. She was, moreover, not simply the "devouring mother" (as so many men fear) or the "whore" as Magdalene was portrayed in Christian iconography. Mamy Wata is *all* of womanhood. At the close of day, the women in Owerri throw their smaller clay icons into the river. Instantly, she goes back to the mud. Isn't that a beautiful metaphor?"

***

"It seems that my dream life has been giving me the clues all along, only the characters were mixed up in so many dreams, but, who knows, perhaps I met them in other lives only in different roles? It is as if I have been on an excavation digging layer through layer and going deeply into all of my many personas. The truth is that BB never betrayed me. I betrayed myself, and our marriage. I looked into the eyes of the "Red Nostril" and the death goddess. From this darkness I tapped into the collective unconscious where, I don't know, how many past lives have brought me to this learning? Who is really dead and who is really alive? This might well be why BB was so afraid. He sensed I would be leaving him and he could not understand it.

"There seems to be a form of psychic dismemberment with this whole process and I have had to go into the dark tunnel to face my own shadow side. How many lifetimes must I learn about? I do not know. Nor do I know how many former lives I have had with BB. Or with Charles Chantel. I only know we have unfinished karma.

"The snake will travel with me, as it is more than an ordinary garden snake, "The snake will not harm you," said the goddess. "My snakes need to be picked up from crawling on the earth and to walk upright with me in a higher place. This will be the task. Go out into the world and teach this lesson. Help to renew energies to heal the earth and one another.

We must move upward to a new understanding of the Great Mother. We will not survive with the hateful divisions and judgments. This time, we must do it correctly. Some women as well as men will try to steal our energy again. Some will try to demonize us again. But the earth must learn to approach both men and women as those people able to aspire into wholeness, and the snake will guide us to a new dawn. We must come out of our long exile. The earth is dying and there is little time left. Without recognizing this cycle of life and death, there can be no change. The chaos is nothing but fear in a sick attempt to control nature. But, paradoxically, it is the very chaos that will help us to heal. BB, I want you to help me.

"I will awaken in another dimension. I will return to my roots. I will be with you. I will follow you like a wave...appearing in many forms, including the snake. We must meet our serpent in the desert and relinquish fear. For what is a snake other than an undulating, pulsating wave motion? The power of the snake will travel with us both. It is always there, always pulsating in the flow of our blood, in the swallowing of our food, in the movement of our intestines, in the rhythm of our orgasms. The snake symbolizes everything that is good and whole within our body, mind and spirit - the snake will be our guide traveling through many lives.

"BB, you must trust me. You will not be hidden from the light, but when you need the darkness you will not be afraid of it. In this way, you will move beyond fears. All masters know this. Never again need we fear Red Nostrils. And in your travels on the sea, you will have the divine power to dive under the surface, and escape the wrecks. Have no fear about a wreck. Swim always towards the shore and take large chunks of green and gold seaweed to nourish you from the ocean's floor. Some day, another time, I will return to you and do so playfully, easily, and you will know. Watch for me in the waves and with the dolphins. In this lifetime, BB, you will find a peace on the sea surrounded by water, and slowly you will learn. You will feel my presence, and you will be able to write our stories. I will be your muse. Remember me always with love, and be faithful to Mamy Wata. This, BB, is what I want you to know.

All my love, always—Your Julia."

Epilogue

IT IS OFTEN STATED THAT any plausible view of reincarnation would have to be written in fiction. Otherwise, in this scientific world of ours, no one would find it believable, even though such beliefs go back to the Egyptians. The precise historical origins of reincarnation doctrines found in the East are difficult to pin down because Eastern philosophy is less concerned with the history and dating of events than the West. The historical sequence of events matters little to those who view life as a repetition of eternal cycles and the physical world as illusion.

As there are endless shades of understanding, reincarnation is known by many names and in Africa it is often known as the "shooting forth of a branch" or "another coming" since it was believed by many that death is an end to one life only and a gateway to another. In all of the creation stories and comparisons of the many traditions, it is a running theme that one must enter the "shadow" of life in order to seek the "vital breath" of light.

With this understanding, we will follow Julia into her other past lives as the cycle of her karmic adventures continues.

Patricia Lee

The End

LaVergne, TN USA
07 October 2010
199853LV00002B/14/P